ICE BLUE

ICE BLUE

LORD & LADY HETHERIDGE MYSTERIES BOOKS #1

EMMA JAMESON

For Donna

CHAPTER ONE

*a*nthony Hetheridge, ninth Baron of Wellegrave, chief superintendent for New Scotland Yard, never married, no children, no pets, no hobbies, and not even an interesting vice, would turn sixty in three weeks. With the exception of his chosen career, his life had largely gone as predicted, without foolishness or significant errors. He had conducted himself with honor, and had even begun to think of himself as one who "held up well" over the years. Growing old did not torment Hetheridge; it was simply part of the graceful arc of his existence. His twenties had been the time for exploration and a thirst for learning; his thirties, for honing his strengths and accepting his weaknesses; his forties, for the cool, self-centered joy only true professional mastery could bring. His sixties would be the natural time of decline—withdrawal into memories, the descending curtain, the snuffed lights. One night, over a gin and tonic, it occurred to him there were dozens of ways to bring down the curtain himself, on his own terms. It was only fleeting, but the idea's hollow cowardice startled him. Rarely these days did anything escape his control, even an errant thought.

Hetheridge had never suffered the torments of the mind that

afflicted his chosen profession, from the greenest constables to his fellow superintendents, who subsisted on takeaway curry and bourbon. Only once, when he was forty-two, had his calm been shaken, when a murder suspect thrust a black, oil-smelling Glock in Hetheridge's face and squeezed the trigger. Before Hetheridge could steady himself, before he could accept the indignity of violent death, there came a deafening crack. He had dropped, unprepared for death, yet unprepared to find himself still alive. The police sniper placed on a rooftop across the street had done his job, felling the suspect before that Glock could introduce Hetheridge's brains to daylight. But daylight, or something like it, had broken in regardless.

For five days he'd been unable to work or receive visitors. One afternoon he found himself sobbing in the walled garden of his Mayfair home—he who loathed displays of emotion, who had no patience for men who acknowledged their innermost weaknesses. He wondered if he could continue to feel on such a level and survive. But on the sixth day his familiar self-control reasserted itself. Fear receded, emotion receded, and he drifted away from that time like a man carried by a swift, smooth current, his life orderly once more.

Now in three weeks he would turn sixty and the sun would set. His legacy: a brilliant career and a spotless reputation. Perhaps he should exit his professional life by retiring on his sixtieth birthday? Nothing was worse than a man who did not know when to take his leave.

Standing before the cherry-framed cheval mirror, Hetheridge knotted his silk tie, waving away alternatives offered by his valet, Harvey. Harvey enjoyed being overly accommodating in every sartorial decision, and Hetheridge enjoyed accepting the first decent option and ignoring the other choices. Harvey had "gone into service," as he put it, to debase himself to a peer, and Hetheridge, resigned to the bizarre effect his title had on a large segment of the population, played along.

Never tall and never handsome, Hetheridge had been mild and boyish in his youth—the eternal "good cop" to his partner's nasty old copper. But time had worked a curious alchemy on his features. His eyes were still bright blue, and his medium brown hair had turned steel gray. But while most of his contemporaries had gone doughy, jowly and soft, Hetheridge had grown into his features. The lines around his eyes and mouth lent an authority his youthful face had lacked. Now there was a firm set to his mouth and a thoughtful crease across his brow.

And I could easily pass for fifty, he thought, enjoying a moment of egotism.

He dressed as he always did—in a beautifully tailored suit, Italian shoes, heirloom cufflinks and a silk tie he'd purchased on Bond Street. His hair, still as thick and coarse as it had been thirty years ago, was trimmed every three weeks to assure perfection. It made little difference how he was perceived as Lord Hetheridge, but a chief superintendent had a certain dignity to uphold.

The crawl of traffic from Mayfair to New Scotland Yard passed as usual, with Hetheridge ensconced in the back of the Bentley, immersed in the *Times* and wishing for a post-coffee cigarette. He had quit nearly twenty years ago, yet the impulse to smoke on the way to the office had never left him, not even for a day.

His driver made the trip with five minutes to spare, and Hetheridge found himself at his destination with the op-ed page still unread. Surprised, he tossed the *Times* on the floorboards and climbed out of the Bentley, blinking in the bright sunshine. He didn't own a pair of sunglasses—in his opinion, sunglasses on the elderly looked ridiculous. But he seemed to need them more each day, he realized, putting up a hand to block the light. A hat was the more appropriate option. Bowler, or wide-brimmed? Pondering this solution as he made his way inside, Hetheridge nearly plowed into Superintendent Vic Jackson, the most recent promotion at the Yard, and Detective Sergeant Wakefield, who were rowing for the benefit of all.

"You're insubordinate!" Superintendent Jackson shouted, face pink with fury.

"You're a plonker!" DS Wakefield shouted back.

Hetheridge, recovering his vision under the blessedly familiar artificial light, took in the rage of each combatant, as well as the avid interest of receptionists, janitors and assorted members of the public. "I say," he muttered, shifting his briefcase from one hand to another.

"I won't have any more insults from you, you dirty little dyke!" Superintendent Jackson bellowed, clearly unaware of Hetheridge's gentle interruption. "Your career is finished!"

"Dyke?" Wakefield screeched. "Because I didn't do you? Because I said no thanks when you pulled out that poor little thing and waved it about?"

My God. Hetheridge stared at DS Wakefield. He'd heard of her, of course, and seen her in passing, across the length of a paved lot. But now he gazed at her as if he'd never seen a woman before. His stomach dropped, as it had when that oil-smelling Glock appeared in his face. *She's beautiful.*

"Clean out your desk." Manhood impugned, Jackson's voice shot into its squeaky upper register. "Get out of my sight!"

"What about Commander Deaver?" Wakefield screamed. "How d'ya fink he'll like fis rubbish?"

"I say, that's enough." Hetheridge's voice rang through the lobby.

The lobby, still electrified by DS Wakefield's defiance, went cold and silent. Her tone, goaded into its extremity, had betrayed the coarse bray of East London.

"This useless mingebag is at fault, sir." Jackson turned to Hetheridge for support. "She—"

"Enough." Hetheridge knew he appeared unruffled, despite the cold rage in his voice.

"Sir, I apologize for losing control. But he—"

"I said, enough," Hetheridge cut across DS Wakefield. Her hair was blond, her eyes hazel, more green than brown.

"I shall speak to Commander Deaver about this unfortunate display," Hetheridge said. "To that end, I require a written explanation from each of you within the next eight hours. In the meantime, no one will suffer another personal insult," he met Superintendent Jackson's eyes, "and no one will clean out their desks," he told DS Wakefield. "And now, if you will accompany me to my office, Detective Sergeant?"

He set a brisk pace to the bank of lifts, aware he was watched by every face in the lobby, and unconcerned. What he felt, or imagined he felt, was the heat of one stare behind him, burning into his shoulder blades as she followed him onto the lift.

Once aboard, he turned, pressed number six and shifted his briefcase from hand to hand. His duty was clear. Superintendent Jackson must be supported. The chiefs and supers always bolstered one another. And beneath that duty, less openly discussed but nonetheless understood, the males of New Scotland Yard always closed ranks against the females. It was nothing against women as a species, of course. Everyone agreed that a pretty face and a soft voice were welcome, as were shapely calves, giggles and a dollop of compassion, when the moment called for it. Hetheridge, who'd rarely been required to work with female officers, had heard all the stories. To hear Commander Deaver tell it, one moment they were all sweetness and light, and the next they rose like cobras, spitting venom about "fairness" and "reciprocity" and accusing every man in sight of sexual harassment.

The lift doors opened. DS Wakefield didn't move. Hetheridge placed one hand so the doors could not close, then gestured, stiff and unsmiling, for her to exit first.

Hazel eyes widened. A smile tugged at her lips, but disappeared into a mask of obedience. She maintained that bland expression as Hetheridge led the way inside.

"Have a seat." Placing his briefcase on the massive credenza, Hetheridge shrugged out of his overcoat, hanging it on the tall stand beside the door. Opening the curtains, he tilted the blinds to let the sun in. Seating himself in his capacious executive armchair, back to the blaze of daylight, he watched DS Wakefield blink, shifting in her far less comfortable seat.

"I say," she murmured, tilting her face away from the glare.

Hetheridge was startled. He hadn't expected her to speak first. Certainly no male subordinate in the same situation would have dared open his mouth before his superior invited him to do so. "What?"

"I say," she repeated, meeting his eyes. "That's how you made the entire room leap to attention. I say," she grinned, the East London accent gone, replaced by a passable imitation of Hetheridge's public school voice. "I don't think I've ever heard that before, except in old movies. These days, it's more like, *oi!*"

"Oi!" Hetheridge shot back, surprising himself with all the menace he could pour into such a basic exclamation.

"Perfect," DS Wakefield crowed. "You could be a football hooligan, sir!"

"Oi," he repeated, warming to her pleasure. "If you imagine a Cockney chimney sweep shouting 'I say!' at someone—sort of an 'Oihgh sah,' you can almost hear it turning into oi, can't you?"

DS Wakefield looked impressed. "I never thought of that. Is that true?"

"Haven't the foggiest." Hetheridge drew a breath. His original stern opening seemed lost forever. "So what was all that then? The row between you and Superintendent Jackson?"

"He's a plonker."

"Naturally. Well, then, I'll inform Commander Deaver. At the Yard, the plonker defense has always been ironclad."

DS Wakefield, perhaps not truly beautiful in the full light of day, was still radiantly pretty, especially when amused. "Or who knows, maybe I'm the plonker." Her eyes were long-lashed and perfectly balanced; her nose and mouth were a tad asymmetrical, making her an individual instead of another nameless lipstick model. "Screaming at my superior officer isn't the best way to make myself understood."

"It sounded like you accused Superintendent Jackson of sexual impropriety."

DS Wakefield studied him silently. Then her face took on that familiar look: mustn't-grumble. "Forget it."

"I see. So you admit the serious allegation you made against Superintendent Jackson, in front of me and numerous others, was a lie?"

"No, sir, it happened. But we were off duty, down at the pub. He was drunk and went too far. I didn't count it against him, not until this morning when he started calling me names."

Hetheridge didn't know what to think. Conventional wisdom —the backroom judgment of his contemporaries—would assume DS Wakefield was choosing to make no fuss at the moment, reserving the right to seduce Jackson later. Commander Deaver would probably argue any impropriety had been consensual, leading her to think she could get away with insubordination the next morning. But did that make sense? And what was it like to be DS Wakefield—young, attractive, intelligent—pursued by a drunken superior with a midlife libido and an unzipped fly?

"I'm sorry," DS Wakefield said, though she neither looked nor sounded apologetic. "Did I shock you, my lord?"

"Here you will address me as Chief Superintendent Hetheridge," he said coldly. He loathed the use of his hereditary title in the Yard, where it was only invoked as a special form of reverse snobbery.

She smiled, eyes sliding away. Something in that slight smile pricked Hetheridge in a way he could not bear. "Yes?"

Silence.

"You have something to say. Go on."

"It's just that everyone calls you 'my lord,' sir. I only said it from force of habit, sir. Sorry, sir."

He stared at DS Wakefield for a long moment. Everything about her phony blandness and gleaming eyes told him it was the truth. In the arena where he prided himself on contending as a self-made man among other self-made men—in the place where brains, drive and courage mattered more than one's forbearers or one's ancestral home—he was mocked as "my lord" by all. Including this woman who'd clawed her way up from the East End, and whose career now balanced on the point of a knife.

"Out of my sight," Hetheridge said, unconsciously echoing Superintendent Jackson. "Write your explanation and have it on my desk by the end of the day. Think carefully about whether you deserve to remain at New Scotland Yard, Sergeant."

She was up in one quick movement, bursting to her feet like a child eager to escape the headmaster's office. Then she paused, mouth twisting, indecision plain on her face. She crossed halfway to the office door, then turned back, pushing her shoulder-length blond hair behind her ears and squaring her shoulders.

"What?" Hetheridge snapped.

"The super and I weren't fighting because he pulled out Little Vic in the pub. Heaven knows I'm used to rubbish like that. We were fighting over a case," DS Wakefield said. "He told me to focus on the dead girl's best client and ignore all the evidence against her boss—motive, opportunity, even a few juicy circumstantial bits. The super made up his mind early on, you see, and wouldn't hear anything that didn't fit his original scenario. That's why he said I was insubordinate. Because I kept up the investigation on my own time. And that's why I said he was a plonker—because he doesn't care what really happened to the dead girl, as long as he stitches up his chosen punter. Superintendent Jackson won't see the truth when it does a strip tease in front of him. That's his problem. I don't suffer fools gladly. That's mine."

Hetheridge digested this information. "What made you finally tell me?"

"I don't know. I had the weirdest feeling you'd listen. I know the top men always prop each other up, especially against women. The lads will boil your bollocks if you don't stand with them. And I know I rub everyone wrong—everyone in authority, at least. Even the women, when I actually encounter one, treat me like a cockroach. But you—there was something in the way you said 'oi!'" DS Wakefield grinned at Hetheridge—a cheeky grin, fearless, bright as the sunlight that had dazzled him when he emerged from the Bentley. "Something like a kindred spirit. So there it is." She grinned again. Then she was gone.

His office door swung gently in her wake, not quite open and not fully closed. Passing a hand over his eyes, Hetheridge reminded himself of his proximity to age sixty and wondered what, precisely, was happening to him.

CHAPTER TWO

*K*ate grasped her mobile phone on the first ring. Hand snaking up from the covers, her fingers closed unerringly around it, flipping it open to silence the noise. Her first thought was absurd: it's Mum, calling for Ritchie. Her next thought was just as foolish: it's Dylan, calling to say he's sorry. If either of these preposterous notions had dared to surface under normal waking conditions, Kate would have stuck her head in a bucket of cold water, or got herself checked for mad cow disease. Strange enough that such fancies occurred to her in the haze between sleep and waking, when her shoulders loosened, her body curled like a child's, and the internal list of promises unmet and aspirations gone stale, flitted away. Maybe, during those few glorious hours, her IQ dropped a hundred points.

"Wakefield," she said thickly, technically awake. It had to be the Met.

"DS Wakefield, sorry to wake you," the female voice said in a perfunctory tone. "There's been a homicide in Belgravia. The Yard has been asked to investigate, and your guv wants you on the scene as soon as possible."

"Fine," Kate said, more awake now, energized by a jolt of surprised pleasure. Superintendent Jackson usually went over the scene himself when it was fresh—the better to form his own unshakable conclusions, without the interruption of another detective's views. Jackson's standard operating procedure had been to call her in the next day, after she had already heard most of the details in the press, and assign her some boring bit of research, like poring over phone records or fact-checking biographies of minor witnesses. Now she was on the case from the first.

"I only need a half hour," Kate lied to the dispatcher, suspecting it might take a full hour to get to Belgravia. "Tell him I'm on my way."

"He's actually on his way to you," the dispatcher replied before Kate could flip the phone closed. "He said he was in the area, and asked for your address. Said he could reach you within a quarter-hour, and the two of you could ride together."

Oh, God, Kate thought, horrified at the idea of Jackson feasting his eyes on her flat. Food-encrusted dishes were stacked in the sink; hampers overflowed with dirty socks and knickers. Not to mention the still-unsolved odor emanating from the bathroom pipes …

"Great. Very thoughtful. Thanks," Kate muttered. She closed the phone, praying the single ring and low-voiced conversation hadn't roused Ritchie.

So Superintendent Jackson had learned her address, and was coming to escort her to the crime scene in his own vehicle. Was it possible, she wondered, sitting up and yawning mightily, that their public row and subsequent interviews with Commander Deaver had actually effected a positive change in the fat-headed old plonker? Or could CS Hetheridge have worked some lordly magic on her behalf?

No, Kate decided, swinging her legs over the side of the bed. Something small and sharp dug into her sole. Suspecting a Lego, Kate kicked it aside, then blinked several times, inspecting the rest of the chilly oak floor for hazards before hurrying to the toilet.

No, she thought again, *if Jackson has changed his approach, it's only temporary, and only until he can find a new way to put me in my place. Is that why he decided to come here tonight? He heard something?*

Kate, fiercely private, had long been terrified her personal life might become fodder for the Yard's gossip. Bad enough that so much of her life—her childhood in and out of care, her schooling, her unlikely rise within the Met—was a matter of public record. Superintendent Jackson had not yet forgiven her for that public reference to his "poor little thing." What revenge might he seek, armed with a few of her secrets?

Determined to be ready the moment the super arrived, Kate barreled into the bathroom, wincing as the fluorescent light above the mirror flickered into blue-white life. A quick inventory of the bathroom was as dire as she'd feared—hair and soap scum lurked in the shower, and the toilet was in need of a good scrub. Well, if Jackson needed the bog, he'd just have to squeeze his knees together. No force on Earth would impel Kate to invite him up to her flat.

Her hair was squashed on one side and sticky with old hairspray. The other side looked almost normal. Sighing, Kate jerked a metal-bristled brush through the sticky side, determined to separate the gluey bits. Then the whole mess would be bundled into a tight bun. With enough bobby pins and with hairspray perhaps she could manage …

"I heard the phone ring." Ritchie appeared in the doorway. At nearly six-one, he loomed over her. Fresh spots had erupted on his left cheek, and his curly brown hair stood out at odd angles. "Heard you talking, too. Going to work?"

"Work," Kate agreed firmly. Rising on her tiptoes, she gripped Ritchie's shoulders and gave him a quick peck, sisterly, on the lips. "But Cassie's here. She'll watch over you until I get back."

"Cassie's asleep," Ritchie said doubtfully. He had never

approved of the tendency of others to sleep while he was awake. Cassie, hired as a live-in carer only two months ago, slept far too much in Ritchie's estimation, and had not yet accrued much leniency with him.

"Yes, and leave her sleeping," Kate said, turning back to the mirror, "unless you really need her. Unless you're absolutely sure you need her. Don't wake her up just to say hello."

"Henry's asleep, too," Ritchie continued, plan transparent on his face.

"Henry especially needs his sleep," Kate emphasized, twisting her hair in a bun. "He has school in the morning. You don't want him to fail his geography test, do you?"

Ritchie shrugged. "I'm bored." He shuffled his feet and glanced behind him, as if someone interesting might have appeared in the parlor. "I miss Dylan."

"So do I," Kate said lightly, rummaging in the medicine cabinet for lipstick and mascara. "Watch some telly, Ritchie. Everyone will be awake before you know it." Closing the bathroom door on him, since Ritchie existed without personal boundaries and would attempt to carry on a conversation no matter what she was doing, Kate plopped onto the toilet and peeked at the cotton crotch of her thong knickers.

Nothing. Clean and spotless.

She glanced at the calendar pinned over the bog roll. Six days late—well, technically seven, since it was now a few minutes past midnight.

I've been late before, Kate told herself, more from bravado than fact. No need to panic. No need to run to the chemist's for a test.

"Dylan," she exhaled—but softly, very softly, lest she disturb Ritchie again, who might even now have fallen back under the spell of his old friend, the telly. "Dylan, where are you?"

* * *

KATE WAS PACING outside her building, trench coat belted against the cold night air, when the silver Lexus appeared, rolling to a slow stop in front of her. The windows were tinted and car's curving lines and flawless finish gleamed under the sodium lights. Kate, who did not recognize the model, an SC 430, and knew the coupe as a Lexus only because of the stylized L in the grille, was impressed nevertheless, and found herself laughing. Who would have thought Superintendent Jackson, plonker extraordinaire, would turn up in such a ride? First an invitation to a still-warm crime scene, and now this? The passenger door swung open, and Kate climbed in, prepared to see Vic Jackson in an entirely new light.

Hetheridge sat behind the wheel in a tuxedo, his black tie unknotted and hanging loose against his crisp white shirt. "Good evening."

"G-good evening. Sir," Kate added hastily, closing the door and fumbling for her seatbelt. "I didn't know you drove."

"From time to time," Hetheridge said mildly, guiding the Lexus out of Kate's neighborhood and merging back into the light South London traffic. "We should be over the river and into Belgravia in ten minutes or less."

"If I'd realized crime scenes in the West End were black tie, I'd have worn a gown and heels."

Hetheridge chuckled. "I was attending a charity ball when the call came in. One of those occasions," he shot a sidelong glance at her, "when homicide is welcome news indeed."

"A charity ball? The charity doesn't happen to operate out of my neighborhood, does it?"

"In the general vicinity. British Youth is planning a new recreational center where a condemned building stands, not far from your home. Good luck that before I left the ball, I checked with the Met dispatcher and discovered you lived just a few streets away. I always do better on the scene with at least one other detective to help catalog the details."

Kate dimly realized that her eight-year-old nephew, Henry, would surely benefit from the youth center's resources while she was at work. But uppermost in her mind was the realization that Superintendent Jackson had not been mentioned. The implication—reassignment—was obvious, yet so sudden, she didn't know how to feel.

"I was expecting Jackson," she said.

"I know." Stopping at a red light, Hetheridge shot her a quick smile. "You've been reassigned. Superintendent Jackson already knows. You were meant to receive formal notice next Monday. But with my other DS tying up loose ends on another case, I decided to bring you aboard early."

"And I'm grateful," Kate said sincerely, fighting hard to stifle a yawn.

He shot her another glance before the light turned green, and the Lexus resumed its course across the Thames. "Let me guess. You have some sort of home life."

Kate laughed. Hetheridge pronounced the phrase "home life" formally and with care, like an alien inquiring after a lifestyle his inhuman intellect could not process. "Afraid so. But when I'm at work, I'm at work. And I'm very glad to receive this opportunity, sir." The phrase sounded equally alien to her own ears, as if she had said the wrong thing. But even if the sentiment was awkward, it came from the heart. Superintendent Jackson had been dead set on keeping her tightly restrained. Perhaps Hetheridge would loosen the lead.

Enlivened by that possibility, Kate continued to study Hetheridge, taking in his usual impeccable grooming, as well as the stylish cut of his tuxedo, until he shot her another quick glance.

"Yes?"

"Oh," she sighed, grinning at him and feeling completely awake. "There's just something about a man in a tuxedo, isn't there?"

He kept his eyes on the road. "Evening dress does counteract a multitude of sins."

Silence, then, as they crossed the river and began navigating the West End. *Geez*, Kate thought, wondering if she would ever manage to conduct an appropriate conversation with anyone in authority. *He probably thinks I was trying to flirt with him. And I doubt he appreciates that sort of thing on the job.*

Part of Kate was relieved. While assigned to Hetheridge, there would be no narratives about heartless wives, no requests to meet him after work at the pub and no male bits making unscheduled appearances, bobbing and drooling for her attention. The other part of Kate thought, *But does this mean he's so correct, I can't make a joke? Can't swear? Can't tell him he's a bloody good-looking old man in his bloody tux?*

"I don't recall," Kate said, diving headfirst into the breach. "Are you married, divorced or widowed, sir?"

This time, the sidelong look was curt. "How is that relevant to our working relationship, DS Wakefield?"

"You mentioned I might have a home life. Now I'm inquiring after yours," Kate replied, unruffled by what she thought of as his Lord Hetheridge voice. It was when he spoke simply, without artifice, that she felt disarmed.

"I never married," he replied in icy tones.

"Oh. Gay. No problem. Works for me," Kate said.

She expected Hetheridge to hook the Lexus right off the road, or at least hit the brakes and launch into a lecture. Instead, he seemed to be holding his mouth firm, and restraining a ripple in his upper body.

"Makes sense," he said at last. "If you resisted Superintendent Jackson's considerable charms, you must be lesbian. If I never made it to the altar, I must be homosexual. Then again," he continued, turning into a neighborhood of wide lawns and imposing façades that Kate had never driven through before, "perhaps you never felt compelled to sample the superintendent's goods, and perhaps I'm a stallion who never found a reason to settle down."

Flashing lights, a lone camera crew from BBC 1, and yards of reflective blue and white crime scene tape awaited them in front of a brilliantly lit, stately brick house. Hetheridge stopped the Lexus, conversing briefly through a lowered window with a PC. Then the police barrier was moved aside, and he was permitted to drive deeper into the crime scene.

Kate was prepared to make some other joke about Hetheridge's status as a stallion—her mind had been working overtime since he uttered the word—but when he cut the engine and turned toward her, his expression quelled all humor.

"This man died a grotesque death. We owe it to him, and to society at large, to find the killer. I expect your best, DS Wakefield. Can you give me your assurance you'll do everything within your power to solve this case?"

As if hypnotized by Hetheridge's gaze and the steady, melodic sound of his voice, Kate heard herself say, "Yes, sir."

"All right, then. Let's get on."

CHAPTER THREE

etheridge parked behind the two-story house, easing his Lexus between a panda car, blue lights endlessly flashing, and a black BMW that surely belonged to the victim, or his family. He had already received a few details from the dispatcher, but did not intend on biasing Kate by revealing them. According to Superintendent Jackson, Kate was a typical flighty female—too distracted by trivialities to home in on the big picture, more interested in personalities than hard facts, and consumed with the desire to solve a big case entirely through her own efforts. Per Jackson's six-page recommendation that Kate be given the sack, her worst failing was wild egotism—trusting too much in her own inexperience while ignoring the hard work and invaluable contributions of steadier, more seasoned detectives. Kate, by contrast, had spent less time crafting her written explanation of the public row with the superintendent. The mandatory report had arrived on Hetheridge's desk with only five minutes to spare before his deadline, scrawled by hand on a piece of copier paper. It consisted of one word: Plonker.

"Your neck of the woods?" Kate looked around the exterior of the detached brick house, with its enormous treed lot and pea-gravel car park, wide enough to swallow the average council flat. "Nice."

"New money," Hetheridge replied, deliberately sounding snobbish. Ordinarily, he would have responded with a shrug, steering any conversation with his juniors away from the personal—especially as it applied to him—to keep their minds on the case. But something about Kate made him want to startle her every chance he got.

"Yes, quite vulgar, really," Kate agreed in a passable imitation of his tone. "This is no murder. Poor bugger must've topped himself from shame."

"Press are crowding the barrier," Hetheridge said, pressing his hand into the small of Kate's back and pushing her forward as photographers shot in their general direction. "Inside. They usually know better than to print photos that include detectives, but it will only take one to compromise the investigation."

He expected her to argue, or perhaps bristle at his touch. He hadn't meant the soft push to be offensive, only imperative, but who knew how the modern career woman might interpret such an action? Hetheridge had never worked with a female DS before, but he had worked with a junior officer whose photo, snapped in front of a corpse and published in the *Sun*, had precipitated the kidnapping and ransom of that officer's wife and child. Hetheridge had no intention of allowing such a tragedy to happen again.

Kate didn't bristle. Obediently, she led them into the house—specifically, into a mudroom, where two uniformed constables awaited them. The room, painted stark white and lit by unshielded bulbs, was home to several metal wheelie-bins, a row of Wellingtons and a pile of dirty trainers. An assortment of macks and trenches were hung at staggered intervals along the rear wall.

"Good evening, Chief," a constable, blond and pale-faced,

greeted Hetheridge. The man looked as if he'd been sick. The sharp stink of vomit hung in the air.

"Good evening, Constable," Hetheridge replied. "This is my partner, DS Kate Wakefield. Where is the victim?"

"Upstairs. Library. Forensic called to say they're held up, but will arrive before dawn. In the meantime ..." The constable handed both detectives filmy blue booties and blue latex-free gloves. Hetheridge covered his shoes, then slipped on the gloves, noting that they were a shade too tight for his hands, and clearly too loose for Kate. Such was the peculiar genius of Met-issued gear: guaranteed to never fit any officer, regardless of height, weight or build.

"The wife, Mrs. Comfrey, blames an intruder. She thinks this was a home invasion. The daughter thinks it might have been a houseguest. The family held a dinner party, but it broke up before the first course was served. Erupted into one big row, according to the daughter, though Mrs. Comfrey says otherwise. Mr. Comfrey went upstairs to the library. Mrs. Comfrey saw the guests off and went up to her room. Around half-ten she went back to the library to check on her husband, and discovered the body. According to her, the French doors on the balcony were open, as if someone broke in that way."

"Or left that way," Kate suggested.

"No sign of forced entry from outside," the constable replied. "The area below the balcony has been roped off, and photos will be taken as soon as it's light."

"Who besides Mrs. Comfrey was in the house when the victim was killed?" Hetheridge asked. Something about family name seemed familiar to him, especially in conjunction with Belgravia, but he couldn't yet place it.

"No one. The daughter, Jules Comfrey, left when the party broke up to go after one of the guests. She said her father had been highly offensive, and she was trying to repair the damage."

"Live-in help?"

"The Comfreys don't have any. When the dinner party was called off, the cook and her helpers packed up the food, cleaned the kitchen and left. We've already taken down names and addresses, and will round them up tomorrow for questioning."

"Is there a groundskeeper or gardener?" Hetheridge asked.

"Yes. Lives in Cricklewood. Takes the train in. He had already left for the day before the guests started arriving."

Hetheridge glanced at Kate. She was taking notes, not on a pad, but on a smart phone, using a stylus with astonishing rapidity.

"Who is being detained in the house now?" Hetheridge asked the constable.

"Mrs. Comfrey and Jules Comfrey. The daughter returned to the house when Mrs. Comfrey called her, after finding the body. Apparently that was her second call, right after 999. They're together now in the parlor. Oh, and Mrs. Comfrey asked to be allowed to ring for her physician. Both ladies are very upset, so I allowed it."

Kate's stylus stopped clicking. She shot a glance at Hetheridge.

"Has the doctor arrived?"

"No, sir."

"Good. Send him away without granting him entry. Furthermore, the Comfreys will make and receive no other phone calls to anyone until I say so. Are we clear?"

"Clear, sir," the constable croaked, embarrassed. He jerked his head at the second constable, who hurried away to make certain the Comfreys' physician was denied access to the crime scene.

"Excellent. Now lead us to the victim."

Taking a deep breath, the pale young constable turned and guided Hetheridge and Kate out of the mudroom, through an old-fashioned scullery and a gleaming white-tiled kitchen, outfitted with every conceivable modern convenience. From there, they entered an oak-paneled corridor dominated by a steep, narrow staircase—the upstairs route intended, in another era, only for servants. At the foot of the stairs, the odor of vomit was sharper, and beneath it lurked two fainter smells Hetheridge knew intimately—the coppery scent of blood, and the sweet, sickening tang of burnt human flesh.

As the constable started up the stairs, Hetheridge paused, gesturing for Kate to precede him. Still engrossed in note-taking, those hazel eyes widened as they had in the lift, when he first insisted on letting her precede him. Then she scooted in front of Hetheridge, ascending the stairs with a quick, light tread. Smiling to himself, Hetheridge followed behind somewhat more slowly, ignoring the twinge of protest from his left knee. Arthritis, he had long ago learned, could only be managed with two things: denial, and an absolute refusal to stop moving.

At the top of the landing, the constable veered right, stopping before an open door. "In here, sir."

Kate, only a meter away from the young man, raised her eyebrows. Hetheridge glanced from the blond constable to Kate, then pointedly back at her, as if inquiring, do you see what I see? The constable, rather slow on the uptake, caught on to Hetheridge's rebuke at last, clearing his throat.

"Sir and ma'am," he corrected. His two-way radio blared, and the constable, looking relieved, turned aside to listen to his fellow officer's question.

Kate was smiling at Hetheridge, eyebrows still raised.

"I don't like to see my junior team members treated with disrespect," Hetheridge said, "male or female."

"Not sure it had anything to do with me being female, at least not this time," Kate replied in the cheeky tone that came so naturally to her. "Not when you swept in with that voice and that ice-blue glare, Lord Hetheridge himself, scaring the stuffing out of everyone, and in a tuxedo, no less. Of course, poor little DS Sod-All faded right into the woodwork." Fitting the smart phone's stylus into its slot, Kate tucked the device into her coat pocket.

"I'll take thorough notes on everything, I promise. But first I want to see the scene, you know, really see it, without trying to distill it into words at the same time."

Hetheridge nodded, hiding his approval. He wanted to see how Kate functioned without influencing her actions. Expression neutral, he gestured once again for her to enter first, then followed her into the library.

Both the library's lamps were still burning. One, an amber-shaded banker's lamp, cast a wedge of light across a rolltop desk swamped with papers. The other lamp, a tall, golden Art Deco torchière, illuminated the center of the room. On either side of the torchière, two leather wingback chairs were placed, facing a brass-screened fireplace. The fire, wood rather than electric, had guttered down to sullen red embers. Crumpled before those embers was a man's body, on its knees before the long marble hearth.

The victim, Comfrey, looked as if he'd died while flailing out of the chair. The victim's hands, loose at his sides, were bloodied and scored with black streaks. Similar marks marred his throat, and black marks scored his shoulders, where his shirt had offered only slight protection. Comfrey was propped against the chair, his head thrown back. Ordinarily a corpse in such a position would fall forward, pulled down by the head's dead weight. In this case, the weapon that had dealt those injuries to Comfrey's hands, chest and neck, a brass poker from the hearth's collection of fire irons, had been driven into his right eye. The poker had been shoved into the skull with enough force to leave it sticking out of the eye socket. And the poker had sufficient heft to keep Comfrey's head thrown back, maintaining his body in the kneeling position, hands loose at his sides like a supplicant.

Hetheridge, absorbing the details of the corpse, nearly missed the soft sound beside him. Glancing over, he took in Kate's ashen face and tight mouth, and knew she had never been exposed to such a crime scene before. Beads of sweat had broken out across her upper lip, and her hands were clenched awkwardly in front of her.

"I need assurance this wasn't a home invasion," Hetheridge snapped, in a tone that suggested Kate had been seriously delinquent. Immediately, her hands unclenched, and her gaze shot to him, startled.

"Examine the balcony. Check behind those curtains and see if the windows have been disturbed. Then go downstairs and inspect the ground beneath the balcony. Determine what tools or physical skills would have been necessary for an intruder to enter from that balcony."

Nodding, Kate moved toward the balcony. It was several paces away, and Hetheridge hoped the fresh air wafting in through the still-open French doors would be enough to steady her. Violent death was hard enough to view, to catalog, to study. But it was the smell of it, the blood and human waste that brought such a death home to Hetheridge, that gripped him viscerally, making him imagine he might actually die the same death, if he contemplated it long enough.

Hetheridge wandered slowly around the room. He kept to a tight path, taking no extra steps and, despite the blue gloves, touching nothing. Until CID finished with the scene, he was hesitant to do anything that might compromise their efforts. Instead, Hetheridge visually inspected the rolltop desk, which was stacked with unopened mail, some handwritten papers and what appeared to be business reports. He examined the small round table positioned between Comfrey's wingback and the torchière lamp. A book had been put there, closed, the reader's place held by a tasseled bookmark. A drink sat beside the book: two fingers of amber liquid in a crystal glass. Both book and glass were spotted with red pinpricks of blood and flecked with what was probably flesh.

Hetheridge turned back to the dead man. Had he been introduced to Comfrey, during one of those endless social obligations, sometime in the last ten or twenty years? The name still nagged at him. Hetheridge, who prided himself on his excellent powers of recollection, hated admitting, even to himself, that he had forgotten something.

Comfrey's face had taken the brunt of the assault. If Hetheridge had ever been introduced to the man, he had no chance of recognizing him now. The man's nose was flattened, hit so often white bone showed through the mess of flesh. His front teeth were broken off. And the smell of burnt skin and hair emphasized the obvious—the killer's poker had come directly from the fire.

Hetheridge had studied the requisite psychology of the homi-cidal individual from books and scholarly papers, as well as from life experience, but in this case, advanced powers of psychiatric deduction seemed unnecessary. This killer was no intruder-stranger. This killer knew Comfrey, and vented his rage—his or her rage, Hetheridge corrected himself dutifully—on Comfrey's face, as killers so often did when the motivation was intensely personal.

Hetheridge glanced at his Rolex. He believed he'd been exam-ining the scene for five to ten minutes, and was startled to learn he'd spent nearly half an hour in the library. The blond constable, whom Hetheridge had nearly forgotten, was still waiting just outside the door, looking strained and eager for dismissal.

"Constable," Hetheridge called, "were you sick in this room?"

"No, sir," the man replied, taking a reluctant step into the library. "I made it outside. It was Mrs. Comfrey, sir. She found the body, was sick, and called 999."

"Of course," Hetheridge said. He took a last look around the library, then smiled at the constable, amused to see that the man did not relax at all. He recalled Kate's characterization of him in his evening dress, sweeping into a murder scene to terrify hard-working young officers. Surely, she exaggerated.

"Take me to Mrs. Comfrey and her daughter, please."

This time, the constable led Hetheridge down the grand staircase, scarlet-carpeted, oak-banistered, and lit by a glittering crystal chandelier. From there, they entered the parlor, a gracious and airy room with modern furniture, mostly white, and bowls of yellow chrysanthemums. Kate stood near the cold fireplace, composed again, tapping on her smart phone. Two women sat on the long white sofa. A slim, angular brunette in her late teens or early twenties, presumably Jules Comfrey, turned toward Hetheridge as he entered. Her face was pale, but he saw no telltale splotches of redness to indicate she'd been crying. Another woman, also brunette but older and softer-faced, glanced at Hetheridge and froze, her hand going to her throat.

"Tony," she cried, rising from the sofa. "Oh, Tony, thank God it's you. Malcolm's dead. What am I going to do?"

CHAPTER FOUR

 ate stopped her rapid-fire notation into her smart phone. *Tony?* she thought, shooting a glance at Hetheridge.

"Madge," he murmured. No reaction, no mirroring of Mrs. Comfrey's instant intimacy—her outstretched hands, her pleading look. Had it not been for Jules Comfrey, reaching up to catch her mother by the arm, Kate thought Mrs. Comfrey would have rushed across the room to embrace Hetheridge.

"Who are you? How did you get in here?" Jules Comfrey demanded, taking in Hetheridge's tuxedo with narrowed eyes and curled lip. She seemed to assume he was a guest from a neighboring house, wandering in to see what all the fuss was about. Kate wasn't surprised by the young woman's irrationality, or her knee-jerk hostility, for that matter. The level of emotion in the room was palpable, sizzling around both women, Jules in particular.

"This is Chief Superintendent Hetheridge, of Scotland Yard," Kate said quickly. "He came directly from a black-tie event to take charge of this investigation."

"Inspector?" Jules looked up at her mother. "Then how do you know him?"

"We were friends, once," Madge Comfrey said softly. The naked pleading in her eyes disappeared, as if Jules's question had recalled her to herself. Face blank, she sagged back down on the sofa beside her daughter. "Forgive me, Lord Hetheridge. When you appeared so suddenly, almost out of thin air, I thought ... I thought I was losing my mind." She gave a short, shrill laugh. "Maybe I am."

"Let's hear your account of what happened, from the start," Hetheridge said, in the same authoritative tone he had used on Kate when she felt herself close to losing control in the library. As he seated himself opposite Jules and Madge Comfrey, Kate's stylus paused. She considered the pair, taking them in not as witnesses, but as women.

Madge Comfrey was about fifty, with thick brown hair arranged in a wavy, gravity-defying halo Kate associated with upper-middle class mavens. Her dress was printed with tea roses and long green vines—Laura Ashley, Kate thought, or one of her imitators. Madge exuded the air of a woman who had once been beautiful, and told herself she still was. Hers was the frozen fore-head and taut, lineless eyes of someone under an aggressive surgeon's care. Her makeup was also a fraction overdone: fuchsia lips, frosted eye shadow, and a thick black line drawn beneath each eyelid.

Under normal circumstances, Jules Comfrey would have been pretty, perhaps even uncommonly lovely. She had precise features, excellent skin, and thick, glossy brown hair that fell to her shoulders. But tonight she was bone-white and trembling with ill-contained fury, fear or both. She was slender enough to look sickly when tired, and her clothes—baggy blue jeans and a rhinestone-accented T-shirt—were poorly chosen, as if she had tried to borrow a bolder girl's style and wound up looking like a poser.

"Begin with dinner," Hetheridge said, settling himself in an overstuffed armchair. "Why did it end prematurely?"

"That was my fault," Madge said. "I had arranged for a small dinner party—two couples and a single friend of Jules's—but Malcolm didn't feel up to entertaining. He asked me to call the whole thing off. But I felt it was too late to cancel. Malcolm didn't take much interest in our guests, I'm afraid, and some of them felt slighted. Everyone decided to take a rain check on dinner and let Malcolm get his rest."

"Rubbish," Jules snapped, not with surprise, but with the triumph of one eager to seize on a lie. "Mother, you can't keep covering for him, especially now. He was a pig and a complete rotter, and he ruined what was supposed to be my night. It wasn't just a small dinner party," she continued, voice rising. "It was my engagement party, and he destroyed it! He treated Kevin like crap and everyone left because no one could bear to be around him for one minute longer!"

"Your father held some animosity toward your fiancé?" Hetheridge asked.

"He thought Kevin wasn't good enough," Jules said, lip twisting into what Kate suspected was a habitual look of disappointment. "He didn't care how I felt or what I wanted. He just wanted a son-in-law who would impress his friends."

"Jules, please," Madge murmured.

"When did the guests leave?" Hetheridge asked Madge.

"Early. Six o'clock, at the latest."

"What did you do as they were leaving?"

"I saw them off, instructed the staff regarding the cleanup of the uneaten food, and left Malcolm to be alone," Madge said, lifting her chin slightly and putting on what Kate could only describe as a brave, insincere smile. All in a day's work, the smile seemed to say. Every wife is forced to overlook some sort of bad behavior from time to time.

"When Malcolm felt under the weather," Madge continued,

"he liked to take a cup of tea up to the library and drink it by the fire."

"Or whiskey," Hetheridge said, expressionless.

"Or whiskey," Madge agreed, still smiling. "My husband wasn't an alcoholic. If he wanted a drink, I never objected." She waited, but Hetheridge seemed content to let the silence stretch out. Jules shifted again, looking more uncomfortable, and finally Madge drew in a deep breath.

"Very well," she said, compelled to fill the silence. "I was angry. I don't deny it. I was disappointed in Malcolm's behavior. I didn't care if he had tea or whiskey, I just left him alone and went up to bed. I fell asleep for a while, until about ten thirty, I think. Malcolm still hadn't come to bed, and that wasn't like him. I decided we'd been angry long enough, so I went to the library to make peace, and found him there. The French doors were wide open, and I knew someone had broken in and killed him. I was sick, I couldn't help it—it was such a shock, I still see him there, whenever I close my eyes. Then I ran away, found a phone and rang 999."

Hetheridge didn't reply. The silence stretched out again, still more uncomfortable and heavy with something unspoken, until even Kate found herself shifting from foot to foot.

"What?" Madge burst out at last. "What else is there to say?"

"This is a large house," Hetheridge said. "But the library and the master bedroom are on the same floor. Not many wives in your situation could sleep soundly from around six in the evening to ten thirty and hear no intruder, no struggle, and no assault."

Madge stiffened. The black-rimmed eyes narrowed; the fuchsia lips pursed. "If you can be bothered to remember, Tony, you will recall I have suffered from insomnia all my life. Valium is the only thing that allows me to sleep. I took some before I retired, after a long day of planning a party that no one, including myself, was permitted to enjoy. You will find the prescription bottle in my medicine cabinet upstairs."

Hetheridge nodded, clearly unperturbed by Madge Comfrey's offense, or her reference to a past when they had been on a Christian-name basis. Studying his profile, Kate tried to imagine when he might have been friends with Madge Comfrey, and precisely how intimate the connection had been. Unlike many of her fellow detectives, she did not find it hard to believe that Hetheridge hid a personal history beyond his biography in *Who's Who*. She could even imagine a sensual side to him, cached somewhere within that wintry exterior. But the idea of him wasting his passion, his lust, on someone like Madge Comfrey, with her stiff halo of waves and her Laura Ashley dress, irritated Kate in a way she couldn't precisely defend.

Hetheridge turned to Jules Comfrey. "What did you do when the guests left?"

"I went after Kevin. He has his pride," she said, shifting in her seat. "There's only so much abuse a man can take."

"How long were you away from the house?"

"Until Mum called me. That was ...," Jules located her mobile in a pocket and flipped it open, scrolling through the call record, "10:49. I came back fast as I could."

"Did you go upstairs?" Hetheridge asked.

Jules nodded. "I don't know why. She told me—told me what he looked like. Told me not to look, that if I saw it, I'd never forget it. But I had to see him. I thought maybe Mum was exaggerating." An awkward smile tugged at her lips. "I thought he wasn't really dead." Crossing her arms tightly across her modest chest, Jules shifted again, as if animated by a dangerous energy that refused to be contained. "And now that I'm sure, I can't really say I'm sorry."

"Jules!" Madge said.

"He didn't care about either of us. He only cared about himself!" Jules screamed at her mother, tears starting in her eyes for the first time. "What if Kevin never forgives me for the way Dad treated him? What if I never get him back?"

Madge Comfrey drew in her breath sharply, but did not attempt to answer. It was Hetheridge who filled the silence.

"Ms. Comfrey, do you think Kevin was angry enough to break into the house and kill your father?"

Jules swung toward Hetheridge. "Of course not!" she cried, her once-pale face growing redder by the second. "And it didn't have to be Kevin. You couldn't throw a stone in Belgravia without hitting someone who hated my father!"

"Jules, you're hysterical," Madge snapped. "You know your father had no personal enemies. He was respected, he–"

"He screwed Charlie Fringate over that shipping contract!" Jules shrieked. "He treated Ginny Rowland like a cheap tart! They came to our house and smiled in his face because he had all the power, but they hated him as much as I did. As much as Kevin did. As much as you did, Mum, even if you're too much of a saint to admit it!"

Madge Comfrey said nothing. Slowly, her eyes slid to Hetheridge's face. Kate saw another glimmer of that pleading look—restrained this time, but present nonetheless.

Hetheridge leaned back in the armchair. He regarded Jules Comfrey for a long moment. Then he stood up, glancing peremptorily at the two constables. "We'll need to locate and speak with the guests, Kevin chief among them. Ms. Comfrey, would you be good enough to supply these gentlemen with Kevin's full name and address?"

"I hope you can find him." Voice breaking into a sob, Jules pulled her knees under her chin, clutching her legs like a desolate child. "Because I sure can't."

CHAPTER FIVE

*H*etheridge left it to the constables to manage the final details—caution Madge and Jules Comfrey not to leave London, escort them to the hotel of their choice, and maintain guard on the house until CID arrived. Once he and Kate were back inside the Lexus, engine started and seat belts clicked into place, Hetheridge turned to her.

"Now. Give me your impressions. Don't try to organize them. Just stream of consciousness."

Kate, who had instinctively flicked on her smart phone, blinked at the small blue-lit screen for a moment, then returned it to her coat pocket. "Is this a test of the relevant details I noticed?"

"More for me than for you," Hetheridge said honestly. "I want to see where we coincide, and where we differ."

"But it will come out unfiltered, and possibly inaccurate …"

"Don't censor yourself. Just begin."

"Right." Kate stared out through the windshield toward the Comfreys' home. It was still lit by flashing blue lights, as well as the reflected white glare around a television news correspondent, reporting from as close to the house as the constables would allow. "Impressions. As far as the crime scene, I think the killer was someone Malcolm Comfrey knew. There wasn't much sign of a struggle. Seems like Comfrey either allowed someone to take a hot poker out of his hand, or else he sat in his chair and watched, unafraid, while his murderer stirred up the fire.

"As far as intruder access—the front door wasn't forced. But the side door, which enters directly into the garage, has scuffs and dents along the bottom, and the jamb is cracked. Someone could have slipped in that way. But the damage looked old, not fresh, like the break-in happened a few months ago and no one bothered to repair it. Neither Madge nor Jules Comfrey knew anything about a break-in. They just said the door was due for replacement."

Kate, apparently unused to any superior allowing her to speak at such length uninterrupted, shot Hetheridge a sidelong glance. In return, he gave her his most neutral look. Even with the case uppermost in his mind, it was amusing to keep Kate off balance, and quite possibly had the effect of making her sharp intellect work even faster.

"What else?" she continued. "Um, right. The Comfreys have an alarm system. But, like most people who live in safe neighborhoods, they didn't turn it on. The Comfreys only arm it when they leave, or after everyone's in for the night. Since it was relatively early, and Jules wasn't home yet, no one set the alarm. So if the killer had keys, he could have let himself in and walked up to the library while Madge Comfrey slept.

"As for the open French doors on the balcony," Kate said, "maybe Comfrey did that himself. Unless the killer brought a grappling hook, I doubt he broke into the house through the balcony. And it definitely looked too far a drop for anyone but Batman to exit that way without breaking a leg. Of course, we'll need daylight and crime scene photos to be sure."

She paused for breath, shot another glance at Hetheridge, and then continued.

"Impressions of the family. Madge Comfrey. Her makeup and hair were perfect. I think she freshened up before the police arrived. Jules Comfrey. Might be anorexic. Something about her isn't healthy. She also wasn't wearing an engagement ring. You'd expect someone in her position to be wearing an iceberg set in platinum. Oh, and …," Kate broke off. "Never mind."

"Uncensored," Hetheridge repeated.

Shrugging, Kate turned that cheeky smile on him. "I think Madge Comfrey expects her previous friendship with you to work to her advantage. Not sure exactly how yet, but she does. That's all. No more impressions. Brain empty."

"Very well." Tires crunching against the pea-gravel car park, Hetheridge turned the Lexus around, then rolled up to the police barrier, waiting as the constables moved to pull it aside.

"I'm going home to change clothes," he told Kate. "I'll expect you in my office at seven o'clock to begin analyzing statements and checking backgrounds. Would you like me to drop you home now, or do you prefer to go directly to the Yard?"

Kate paused. The correct answer, for an eager junior officer on her first major murder case, was obvious: just fling me out near the Yard's revolving sign, guv'nor, and I'll fortify myself on stale coffee and nicotine until I've obtained a full confession and a commendation from 10 Downing Street. Hetheridge sensed that Kate wanted very much to give him that answer, and prove what a good chap and a hard-charging lad she really was, but that something in her private life made such single-minded careerism impossible.

"I need to go home," she said at last. "Tie up some loose ends. But I'll be ready to work at seven, I promise."

Nodding, Hetheridge steered the Lexus toward the river, and South London. It was still shy of three o'clock, and serene along the open highway—the endless, soul-shriveling crawl of morning traffic wouldn't happen for at least another two hours.

"So," Kate began, that satisfied needling tone creeping back into her voice, "what exactly was the nature of your friendship with Madge Comfrey, Chief?"

Hetheridge repressed a smile. He had expected this, and was prepared. "How precisely is that relevant to you, Sergeant?"

"I like to be as thorough as possible when evaluating person-alities, sir."

"I told you she was once a friend. We lost touch completely, as you may have guessed. That should be sufficient to satisfy your professional interest."

"Sauce for the goose should be sauce for the gander," Kate said.

"Meaning?"

"Meaning if I were the one who had a prior connection to an individual who, frankly, has to be considered a prime suspect, you would require complete transparency on my part. If this fiancé of Jules's, for example, was an ex-boyfriend of mine, I don't think you'd let me escape with a blanket statement that our liaison is over, thank you, and no further questions are allowed."

Hetheridge shot a glance at Kate, startled by her candor, which hovered just below outright insubordination. He had experience dealing with insubordination. This was also the truth, and its simple clarity had thrown him. Now he was the one off balance.

"Very well. I was once engaged to Madge Sowerby, as she was called then. More than twenty years ago, I might add, so the jury is out as to whether you were even alive at the time. The engage-ment ended, the friendship cooled, and we went our separate ways."

Kate turned toward him, unabashed interest in her face. "Who broke the engagement?"

Hetheridge was so surprised by her audacity, he actually grinned. "Before I answer that, Sergeant, I look forward to hearing how such a detail could be relevant to Malcolm Comfrey's murder."

"It isn't," she grinned back, delighted. "I just want to know."

Hetheridge, at a loss, faltered in his route, nearly missing the turn to cross the river. He was pleased by her personal interest in him. Pleased, embarrassed by that pleasure, and strangely willing to endure the embarrassment if he could extend the pleasure a little longer.

Correcting his route and narrowly accomplishing the turn, he replied, "I was the one to break it off. She didn't forgive me, which is probably to be expected."

"Why did you end it?"

"I realized I didn't want to be married," Hetheridge replied with utter honesty. "Especially to her."

"Did you tell her that?"

"Good God, no. I told her I wasn't good enough. That she deserved a man who wasn't already married to his work." Even by the dashboard's subdued glow, Hetheridge could see Kate was waiting for more. "I have managed to associate with a few other women over the years. Would you like me to list them alphabetically, or in order of importance?"

She chuckled. Hetheridge, prompted by his rising embarrassment to change the subject, impulsively posed a question he'd thus far denied himself permission to ask. "So, who are you going home to? A boyfriend? A fiancé?"

"A brother," Kate said. Her voice held a note of finality, as if the subject was off-limits. Hetheridge had heard this about her—heard she guarded the details of her life outside the Yard like a dragon—and was prepared to let the question drop. Although he pried for a living, collecting secrets and violating privacy to a degree the typical village busybody could only fantasize about, Hetheridge was always correct in personal interactions. He loathed the idea of forcing a confidence.

"A brother who gets very worried when I don't check in on him," Kate continued, giving Hetheridge a new sort of smile—a vulnerable smile, hinting of trust. "He's intellectually challenged, as we say now. Mentally retarded. Ritchie has a live-in carer, but he still needs me. If I went off in the middle of the night and didn't come back for a day or two, he'd go to pieces. I also have a nephew, Henry. He's one sharp little guy," she said with pride. "He's eight, but most of the time he behaves like an older brother to Ritchie. If I just make Henry's breakfast and give him a kiss goodbye, he understands completely. Henry was only supposed to stay with me for a month, but somehow the arrangement turned permanent." She stopped. Taking a deep breath, she put on a broad, false smile. "Let me guess. More than you wanted to know?"

"More than I expected you to tell," Hetheridge said. "Quite the family life."

"Quite the buggery bollocks of a family life," she snorted, the false smile disappearing. "Sometimes I hate being home and I love the Yard to an obscene degree—a gibbering, drooling, insane degree. When I get that way, I feel my work is my reason for being alive, and I love it. Other times, I come home to Ritchie and Henry, and we have a fun dinner and a few laughs, and I go to bed thinking they're the absolute best things in my life. But neither feeling sticks around for long."

Hetheridge, unwilling to make insincere small talk about a situation he could hardly imagine, said nothing. They settled into an easy silence, journeying over the river and back into South London, neither compelled to speak until Hetheridge pulled up in front of Kate's building.

"You remembered how to get back without turning on the GPS," Kate said, unbuckling her seat belt.

"Detective," Hetheridge said, touching his forefinger to his temple.

"See you at seven." Climbing out of the car, Kate reached up to undo her tight bun, pulling her hair free in thick, matted strands. She closed the car door behind her, took a step toward her building, and then turned back, opening the door again.

CHAPTER SIX

$\mathcal{K}$ate made it back to New Scotland Yard by 7:03 a.m. Hurrying into the lobby with breakfast, a large coffee heavily dosed with artificial sweetener and creamer gripped in one hand, she swerved around two human roadblocks and made for an open lift.

"One more!" she called to the navy blue suits and frowning faces that occupied the half-empty lift. No one moved, and the doors began to close.

"Wankers," she muttered, throwing herself toward the lift. Her left hand shot into the shrinking space between doors and wall, and the mechanism halted, opening again. Kate's shoulder bag rocketed backward as she entered, smacking the nearest navy-suited man, and the slick bottoms of her pumps threw her off balance, almost sending her into the arms of a scowling, thin-lipped woman. Relieved to still be in custody of her coffee, Kate repositioned her handbag, corrected her posture and smiled at her reflection in the lift's highly polished metal doors. She'd worn her best suit—a gray pinstriped jacket/skirt combo with a hint of pink in the weave, and a bit of black lace peeking out at the cuffs and hem. She'd even gone so far as to wear those hazardous black pumps, which were already pinching her toes. She looked pulled-together, competent, professional.

"Tarted up for your next conquest?" a voice said in her ear.

She half turned to see Superintendent Jackson, one of the navy suits, directly behind her. His face looked fatter than ever. A crumb of something white, probably pastry, clung to the corner of his moist pink mouth.

"Just on my way to Hetheridge's office," she said sweetly.

Jackson snorted. "He's gone soft in more ways than one. Tough sell for the likes of you."

The lift dinged, and the doors opened on Kate's floor. Crossing the lift's threshold, she put her shoulder against its retracted doors and fixed Jackson with a pleading look.

"Now that I've been reassigned, I just want to take a moment and publicly ask your forgiveness for saying you had a small penis. A man's penis size should never be mocked in the workplace. And the way I squeezed my fingers together to indicate something itty-bitty, or just stuck out my pinky finger to symbolize you," she continued, demonstrating both actions, "was inexcusable. Please forgive me, and understand I've learnt my lesson." With that, Kate released the doors and stepped back. The doors shut, and Superintendent Jackson's spluttering curses traveled toward the next floor up.

Kate regarded the closed doors for a moment, beginning to blush, as she always did after an impulsive act of defiance. He'd make her pay for that, sooner or later, and probably in a way she could ill-afford. Why did she have to rise to his baiting? Why couldn't she have the restraint of, say, Hetheridge?

Because I'm not him. I'm Kate, she sighed inwardly, taking a swig of coffee and hurrying toward the chief's office. *And if he'd lived my life, he'd be a wee bit snappish, too.*

She paused before entering the office, tossing her half-full cup in a corridor rubbish bin, and trying on a calm, professional expression. No good looking more interested in sucking down her breakfast than in getting down to business on the Comfrey murder.

Opening the door, she made her way from the reception area, where the administrative assistant's desk sat empty, toward Hetheridge's office, and the glorious aroma of bacon and eggs.

A pleasant-faced man in his mid-thirties sat in a chair pulled up to Hetheridge's wide desk, chomping contentedly on bacon and fried bread. He was dressed in a blue striped shirt with white collar, black vest and black trousers. His thick hair was glossy black, his complexion dark, and his eyes looked as black as his hair. Kate had glimpsed him around the Yard from time to time, but still had to look at his ID to recall his name.

"DS Bhar?" she asked, pronouncing it carefully. His first name was Deepal.

"Call me Paul." Wiping his hands on the linen napkin in his lap, he put out a hand to shake. "Sit yourself down. Always another space at the trough."

Kate grabbed a chair and dragged it close, placing her handbag on the floor and awkwardly crossing her legs at the ankles. That was the worst thing about her best suit—the skirt was exactly the wrong length to sit comfortably. "The chief mentioned you last night. Said you were wrapping up another case."

"Wrapped," Bhar said with satisfaction, popping another piece of bacon in his mouth. "This case is way more interesting, anyway. Murder in Belgravia. That's what they'll call the minis-eries. And I always fancied being interviewed on telly, explaining the mind of the super-rich killer. Now eat. Seriously. Don't force me to become fatter than I already am."

Kate smiled at Bhar, neat and trim despite his rapid style of consumption, and studied the spread on Hetheridge's desk. "This is amazing."

Before her, in silver serving dishes, the traditional English breakfast waited: eggs, bacon, sausages, mushrooms, fried bread and kippers. A tall silver coffee pot sat to one side, with a single remaining china cup beside it.

Happy to cave in, Kate loaded up the china plate someone had provided for her, digging into everything except the kippers. Then she poured a cup of coffee, doctoring it with real sugar and half-and-half before savoring a mouthful. It tasted like the beans had been ground fresh before brewing.

"Who provided this?"

Bhar shot her a knowing looking. "Lady Hetheridge," he stage-whispered.

Kate blinked at him. Before she could ask, Bhar gave some sort of awkward signal, like trying to point with only his shoulder, and bent his head to his breakfast.

Hetheridge's administrative assistant, Mrs. Snell, entered. Kate knew that most of the Yard, including the senior officers, were terrified of her. She was a tall, scrawny woman with protruding collarbone, nonexistent bosom, and wide, accusing eyes. Her hair was a fierce white, set in waves that would have looked outdated thirty years before. Her style of dress, high-necked with a hem falling to mid-calf, could only be described as somewhere between the Queen and Dame Edna Everage. No one knew Mrs. Snell's age, which fell between sixty and eighty. No one asked her questions—she asked the questions, and invariably received answers.

"How is breakfast?" she demanded in a crisp, headmistress sort of tone.

"Excellent," Bhar mumbled, mouth full of egg.

"V-very nice," Kate said, stammering in spite of herself.

Mrs. Snell's eyes narrowed behind her large lenses. "I hope," she said suspiciously, "there will be no problems, now that you have joined us, DS Wakefield?"

Kate found herself speechless—a sparrow enthralled by a cobra. Bhar poked her in the leg with his foot.

"N-no," Kate quavered. "I'm grateful to be part of the team."

Mrs. Snell studied her in cool disbelief. Then, drawing herself up, she said, "Good," in a skeptical tone and exited the office, presumably returning to her own desk.

"Oh, God," Kate said, turning to DS Bhar and shuddering in relief. "She's ghastly."

"She's someone you'd better learn to please, if you want to survive with the old man," Bhar cautioned. "She irons his shirts when he pulls an all-nighter. She chooses his dinner when he works past eight. I heard she and his 'manservant,' Harvey, got into a hissing, hair-pulling catfight when ..." Bhar broke off again, sitting up straight and smiling as the office's door reopened. "Sir," he cried, hitting a grand, false note as Hetheridge appeared, "great to see you."

"Good morning," Kate said, her sausage pausing on the way to her mouth. Was she supposed to stop eating, now that he'd arrived?

Hetheridge had changed from his tuxedo into his usual attire —smartly cut suit, silk tie, polished Italian shoes. He looked rested, as if he'd enjoyed a full eight hours' sleep, though she doubted he'd had any.

"Do continue," he said with a slight smile, coffee cup in one hand. "Mrs. Snell is cross when her breakfast offerings are neglected."

"Oh, sir," Bhar said, adopting a sinuous Indian accent quite different from his usual way of speaking, "since I came to this country, I have begged and prayed for a woman. And now, at last, you grant my request. When may I marry and beget my dynasty on this fertile female?"

Hetheridge dropped into his black executive armchair, studied Bhar for a moment, then turned to Kate. "Moving on. Any fresh insights into the scene last night? I've already written up a preliminary report and given it to DS Bhar to read."

"Gripping stuff," Bhar breathed, returning to his normal manner of speaking, and placing his empty plate on

Hetheridge's desk. "It moved me as no writing has moved me before."

Kate repressed a giggle. She could see the amusement buried in Hetheridge's eyes, and wondered if Bhar could, too. Or would he keep going, riffing in new and absurd ways, until he made his superior laugh out loud?

"Almost moved my bowels," Bhar added.

"Thank you," Hetheridge said repressively. "DS Wakefield. Last chance to add anything before I give you a copy of my report, and determine assignments for the day."

"I'd like to track down Jules Comfrey's fiancé," she replied. "Also the guest named Fringate, the one she said her father screwed on a business deal, and that Rowland woman – the one she said her father treated like a tart. For that matter, I'd like to speak with Jules Comfrey herself. Her mother silenced her a few times last night. I think she might say more on her own."

"I intend to re-interview Jules Comfrey myself today," Hetheridge said. "And Madge Comfrey, too, but not until Forensic Services has results for us. Good observation about her hair and makeup looking fresh, Wakefield. I called Forensic Services and asked them to check the pipes of every sink and shower for evidence of blood and human tissue. Also asked them to check every outdoor dustbin in the neighborhood, not just the Comfreys'."

"And Forensics told you?" Bhar asked.

"To mind my own business and let them get on in peace," Hetheridge grinned. "But Forensics, as we know, will sometimes cut corners in a house that large." He took a sip of coffee. "They're under tremendous pressure right now. First to solve every crime from nothing but a wad of chewing gum and a partial shoe print, the way forensic teams do on television. Yet also to spend less money, and justify the number of special tests run. Knestrick is our man this time, and he would have been content to only examine the library, balcony and front door, if he could get away with it. He wasn't happy to be asked to dismantle the house's entire plumbing system, more or less, but he'll do it, since I could link the request to a specific investigator's observation."

Kate put her own empty plate on top of Bhar's. "If I may ask, sir, why do you want to handle the Jules Comfrey interview personally?"

"Belgravia," Bhar hinted.

"There has already, if you can believe it, been a certain amount of pressure brought on our unit," Hetheridge replied. "These are the sort of cases that always come to us. The expectation from the top, and from other offices within the government, is that I will handle it with a minimum of fuss. And, I might add, with zero complaints from any influential people who might be touched in the course of the investigation."

"Can't have Kate Wakefield bulldozing in, being impertinent and working her betters into a froth," Bhar said.

"I understand," Kate sighed. "But is there any way you could give me a chance with Jules? I really think I'm the better choice, sir."

Hetheridge regarded her levelly. "Why?"

"Because I'm female, and not too far from her age. Because I'm not married," Kate said. "Because there's something odd about the fact she wasn't wearing an engagement ring, yet she claimed her father ruined her engagement party. She also mentioned that Malcolm Comfrey didn't think her fiancé was good enough for her. I have a feeling dear old Dad might have been right about that. I can't see Jules Comfrey telling you—a man who will probably remind her of her father, if you'll excuse me for saying so, sir—about her boyfriend troubles. But she might tell me."

Hetheridge said nothing for a moment. He put down his coffee cup and leaned far back in his chair, which creaked in protest. "You're right," he said at last. "Very well. Bhar and Wakefield, I'd like you to work together today. Interview Jules Comfrey, Charlie Fringate and Ginny Rowland. If the PCs succeed in rounding up the fiancé, Kevin, I'd like you to interview him, too. Report any breaking details directly to me. Otherwise, we'll meet again this time tomorrow. And remember, Wakefield—go softly with Jules Comfrey. I see enough of Commander Deaver as it is."

CHAPTER SEVEN

"Care if I drive?" Bhar asked Kate. "I have a new car. Still has that smell."

Kate shrugged, pleased to escape the duty of navigating what would still be rush hour traffic. Following Bhar to the car park, she smiled at his shiny Vauxhall Astra Elegance, dark blue with sleek detailing and a spotless black interior.

"No food, no smoking," Bhar said as he released the passenger door's lock. "This vehicle will remain clean. Each time we exit, you will collect any blond hairs clinging to the headrest. Before each reentry, your shoes will pass visual inspection."

"My Lord wasn't nearly so fussy about his Lexus," Kate said, inhaling the new car scent with pleasure.

"My Lord has enough money to buy himself a new toy whenever he wants. This," Bhar said proudly, buckling himself in and starting the engine, "represents a large chunk of my compensation package. It also represents my desirability to London's dateable population. It must remain perfect."

"How long since you've had a date?" Kate asked.

"Two months," Bhar sighed. "Might as well be taking the bus."

Putting the car in reverse, he asked, "See much of Superintendent Jackson since the big blowup?"

"Heard about that, did you?"

Bhar laughed. "I have the inside line on it. My source, who is absolutely unimpeachable, actually overheard the confrontation between Jackson and Hetheridge. Most of it came right through the office door. Hetheridge can really roar when someone tries to shout over him."

Kate, who had no friends at the Yard, and no sources of any kind, squirmed. She had assumed Hetheridge simply read Jackson's report, not to mention her ridiculous one-word reply, which she still regretted, and recommended she be transferred. She'd never imagined any conflict between the two men, and had seen no sign of it, unless Jackson's reference to Hetheridge "going soft" was an indicator. But the men of the Yard spent so much time questioning one another's potency, Kate hadn't found the dig unusual.

"What did your source overhear?"

Bhar, who had traveled only a few meters, pulled into another spot and parked again, engine still running. This story was apparently too juicy to relate without gesturing with both hands.

"Well, you can imagine Jackson's side. He took you to a pub to make you feel like one of the boys. You came onto him, he's only human, but the moment he showed interest, you screamed sexual harassment. The old man said you didn't scream harassment, you screamed 'plonker.' Jackson shouted that just proved his point—what happens off-duty has nothing to do with what happens on the job. Then Hetheridge started booming like Zeus." Bhar grinned at Kate. "He said lascivious public behavior is bad form for a family man. He said seducing a subordinate is bad business for a superintendent. And then," Bhar finished triumphantly, "he said it was no way to treat a lady."

Kate goggled at him.

"Yes! That's how I looked! My face, exactly like yours! Sure, whipping out old one-eye is no way to treat a lady—but what does that have to do with a brass-knuckled bitch like Kate Wakefield?" Bhar cackled. "Anyway, Jackson went crying to Commander Deaver, the commander called Hetheridge behind closed doors, and *voilà!* Here you are. The old man went against the brotherhood for you."

"Oh," Kate breathed, feeling unworthy of the sacrifice. "I told him they'd boil his bollocks."

"I said something similar," Bhar agreed, his tone slightly more serious. "Mentioned a hazard down south, at the very least."

"What did he say?"

"He said his bollocks are steel, and let them do their worst. I'll admit, I'm impressed. He really does have a soft spot for you. Pretty soon, you'll be as enamored of him as batty old Mrs. Snell. She thinks he's a sexy beast." Bhar was still smiling, but there was something appraising in his dark eyes. "Who knows, maybe you do, too."

Kate didn't know how to answer. "You're pretty good at questioning," she said at last. "Want to take Charlie Fringate, once I'm finished with Jules Comfrey?"

"Love to," Bhar said, backing out of the space and steering them toward the long line of morning traffic. "And don't worry. You're not the first wide-eyed DS to fall under His Lordship's spell. He covered for me once, when I made a bloody stupid mistake and almost torpedoed a triple murder case. I was so grateful, I wanted to have his baby."

"What stopped you?" Kate giggled.

"Turns out I'm straight. Also, male. But it was a dreamy romance while it lasted. By the way," Bhar shot her a quick glance, "no offense about the brass-knuckled bitch remark. I meant it as a compliment."

"I took it as one."

"I live in hope that one day," Bhar continued, "people will speak of me and say, that Paul, he's one ruthless, cold-blooded bastard. Instead of, that Paul, he's such a nice young man, I can't imagine why he chose such a violent profession."

The trip to Madge and Jules Comfreys' hotel, a glass-and-steel tower overlooking Green Park, was nearly an hour's crawl between traffic lights. Once in the lobby, they showed their warrant cards to a manager, who phoned up to Jules's suite. He stared at Kate and Bhar as he waited for Jules to answer, a skeptical, not-with-my-guest-you-don't expression on his face.

"I'll be back," Kate told Bhar, and went off in search of the ladies'.

Inside the stall, Kate couldn't resist scrutinizing her thong's cotton crotch, still hoping for a sign that her period had straggled in to save the day. Nothing.

Sighing, she did her business and then continued to straddle the toilet, counting backward to the last time she and Dylan had sex. It had been their only unprotected coupling in two years—make-up sex, hot at first, but then cooler, and finally embarrassingly out of sync. After what seemed like an interminable effort, Dylan managed to complete the act, triumphing over what Kate's plainspoken grandmother called distiller's droop. Kate had been relieved to roll over and feign sleep. Hard to believe their once intensely physical, almost entirely sexual connection had vanished not with a bang, but a whimper.

Harder to believe, Kate thought with a stab of real fear, that such a lousy final attempt at intimacy might have left her pregnant.

Kate made her way to the row of porcelain sinks, studying herself in the gilt-framed mirror. She was being ridiculous. She could call Dylan. She could call him right now, just to touch base.

Kate didn't go for the phone tucked in her handbag. Instead, she washed her hands slowly, wondering why she'd kept Dylan

Corrigan in her life for two years. Maybe because he was every-thing she liked: dark hair, blue eyes, sarcastic wit, and a broody set to his mouth and eyes. He always looked as if he were pondering the ways the world had failed him, and formulating terrible cutting remarks to make himself feel better. Dylan's body was nothing special, skinny and pale, but she'd adored the smell of him, the feel of him, how they entwined together. That was what had kept her from chucking him out long ago—their word-less skin-to-skin connection, superior to any interaction that required conversation, teamwork or sacrifice.

Dylan, a sometime-clerk in a New Age store, was also a musi-cian—a guitarist between bands, when Kate met him. He read highbrow up-to-the-minute literature Kate found difficult to understand and impossible to enjoy. He listened to experimental music exclusively from up-and-comers who never lived up to his predictions of success. An insomniac night owl, Dylan got on well with both Ritchie and Henry, content to keep the boys company whenever Kate was working a case. But he had little respect for Kate's career at the Met. To his mind, she was only a cog in the government machine, agent of a socially corrupt system. Dylan was an anarchist at heart, or so he said, but not enough of an anarchist to refuse his dole money. Most of his crit-icism of the "establishment," she'd finally realized, came down to criticisms about her, and how she chose to live.

If he'd only been willing to try and contribute, Kate thought. It never mattered to her that he didn't earn much, either as a store clerk or a musician. The amount he brought in wasn't the point. She only wanted him to acknowledge what it cost to run a household—what he spent on Guinness and pub chow and eBooks—and give something back, not just take. Dylan had accused her of trying to bully him into the middle class respectability that someone like her, climbing out of an impover-ished childhood, craved. When they fought, he insisted she wanted him to become a drone bee, just like her, so she wouldn't regret her own conventional path. As their fights worsened, he'd spent more time out of her company, drinking heavily, hanging out with single friends, and—she suspected—auditioning new, less demanding females.

The rubbish I took off him, just to come home to a man in my bed, Kate thought. *And not much of a man, at that.*

She pressed her fists against closed eyes, refusing to cry, to accept the heat of a single tear. Dylan Corrigan was far from the first male to fit her own inexplicable preference. Every boyfriend before him was a variation on the same genotype. Smart, lazy, full of clever excuses, with a weakness for spending other people's money. The attraction always started with sexual electricity, evolving into a twice-a-day, can't-get-enough-of-him affair that gave Kate the verve to take on whatever the world tossed at her. But when the ardor faded—when the conversations became strained, when she realized she didn't respect him, and he didn't even like her—Kate always found herself looking for a new variance on the same lover. Perhaps she lacked the ability to sustain a true relationship with another human being. At least she could sustain passion, and she'd learned to get by on passion alone.

What if she was knocked up? What if she'd done what she'd sworn never to do, when her sister announced she was pregnant with Henry? And with a man Kate was finished with, who no longer stirred the slightest tenderness in her, who would never be out of her life if she gave birth to his child?

Of course, giving birth wasn't the only option. But Kate's history of failed relationships made her wonder if this might be her only chance to have a child. What if her career took off? What if the next ten years passed even faster than the last ten, and she found herself wondering why she hadn't considered single motherhood while she could?

Taking a deep breath, Kate straightened her shoulders, smiled at herself in the mirror and pushed the whole mess out of her mind. Time to work. Time to interview Jules Comfrey. *And maybe*, Kate caught herself thinking with a twinge of guilt, *her man problems are even worse than mine.*

CHAPTER EIGHT

uniformed porter escorted Kate and Bhar up to Jules's suite. Madge Comfrey opened the door.

"Jules is still getting dressed. Come in," Madge said in a dull, rigidly controlled voice. She ushered them into the floral-wallpapered sitting room, where a loveseat, two striped armchairs and a small coffee table awaited them.

Madge Comfrey looked ten years older than she had the night before—only twelve hours ago, Kate realized. She had changed into simpler attire—a gray turtleneck, black slacks and no jewelry, except for her wedding band. That stiff halo of wavy brown hair had deflated, and her makeup was dry and flaky. Her fuchsia lips stood out against her white face.

"I'm surprised you haven't come to question me again," Madge said. "I expected it to be me, not Jules."

"We're obligated to be very thorough, Mrs. Comfrey. Not only to apprehend your husband's killer but to make sure the charges stick," Kate said. "Many interviews will only be a formality. We'll be speaking to each person who saw Mr. Comfrey in his final hours, just to make sure no piece of evidence is overlooked."

"But surely you aren't just wasting time chatting with us?"

Madge demanded, apparently incensed by the standard reassuring script Kate had quoted from Scotland Yard's playbook. "Surely there must be a scientific effort going on to identify the person who invaded our home? Fingerprints, DNA, security cameras—I'm sure half our neighbors have them—all those avenues are still being explored, aren't they?"

"Of course." Bhar flashed Madge his boyish smile. "Every case gets solved by Forensic Services, just like on the telly. But detectives still have to conduct interviews and take statements. It's standard operating procedure, nothing to worry about."

Madge looked unconvinced. "Are you sure you wouldn't rather talk to me?" she asked, casting a quick glance over her shoulder and lowering her voice. "Jules is very naïve. She's just lost her father. I don't want her to feel browbeaten and attacked by the police, too."

"We'll treat her with every courtesy. CS Hetheridge was very clear on that point," Kate said, wondering what effect Hetheridge's name would have on Madge.

No flicker of response passed over Madge's pale, overpainted face. "Very well, then. I have a great many calls to make, and arrangements to oversee. I'll be in the bedroom if Jules needs me," she murmured, and retreated deeper into the suite.

Jules entered the sitting room less than a minute later, dressed in another pair of calculatedly ripped jeans and a black T-shirt emblazoned with the words KEVIN'S TOY. Kate had seen such personalized tops, sold in the back of celebrity magazines, but she'd never come face to face with a grown woman willing to wear one.

"Sorry I kept you waiting," Jules yawned, covering her mouth and waving for Kate and Bhar to be seated. "I can't seem to pull myself together. This feels like a dream."

Jules shook Bhar's offered hand as he introduced himself, then belatedly recognized Kate. "Oh, it's you. Guess you haven't slept, either. Did you find Kevin?" she asked, apparently believing detectives from Scotland Yard had spent the night beating down doors and vaulting from rooftop to rooftop in search of her man.

"The police are still looking," Kate said. "I take it he hasn't tried to get in touch with you?"

"No, and I've called him a hundred times," Jules said, pulling her mobile phone from her jeans pocket and placing it on the coffee table. "I've called his mum, his sister, the place where he used to work. Nothing. Daddy really managed to fix things," she said, her face settling into that habitually disappointed mask Kate had noticed the night before. "Couldn't even get killed without killing my happiness, too."

"Tell me about the engagement party," Kate said. "Had you been planning it for a long time?"

"Only a week or so. It was mum's idea. She liked Kevin much more than Daddy did. She thought a party with just a few guests would help ease Kevin into the family."

"You mentioned your father didn't like him. Is that why you aren't wearing your ring?"

Jules glanced at her left hand, then covered it with her right—a gesture so quick, it might have been reflexive proof of an embarrassment her conscious mind refused to admit. "We haven't picked out a ring yet. That's Kevin and me. Material things always come last for us."

"When's the big day?" Kate asked, betting she already knew.

"Haven't settled on that, either. The big decision's made. Everything else is a minor detail."

Oh, Dylan, Kate thought, recognizing the shadow of doubt in Jules's large blue-gray eyes, *whoever keeps cloning you needs to stop, or an entire generation of women may go off men*. Smiling at Jules, she decided to take a gamble.

"So what are his best qualities? What made you ask him to marry you?"

The doubt vanished from Jules's gaze. She smiled back. "I've never known anyone like Kevin. He's an artist, and very intense.

But at the same time he has a hidden side, a vulnerable side, he won't let anyone see. Of course, he's good looking, and amazing in … other ways," she giggled, throwing a glance at Bhar. "And it wasn't just me asking him to get married," she added, suddenly realizing what she'd revealed. "He wanted it, too, but he didn't know how to say it. I had to make the first move, because he's so insecure, deep down. He kept telling me I was too good for him, and I deserved someone who wasn't married to his work."

Isn't that what Hetheridge told Madge Comfrey, right before he broke their engagement? Kate wondered. *Do all men use the same excuse when they're desperate for a way out?*

"Tell me again about the two couples your mother invited to the party," Kate said, consulting the notes in her smart phone. "The first guest you mentioned was Charlie Fringate. You said your father cheated him over a shipping deal."

"Yes, that was Daddy's business. Global freight and cargo. Last year, Charlie was going through a rough patch with his company, and he needed a good deal on overseas shipping rates to turn a profit. Daddy promised him a certain rate and changed his mind at the last minute. Charlie lost a ton of money, and I think it ruined their friendship. But Charlie still came around the house. He needed Daddy much more than Daddy ever needed him." Jules paused, transparently holding back something—something she wanted to say.

"And if you hear a rumor about Charlie and Mum, ignore it," Jules said at last, releasing her breath in a rush. "It's not true."

"A rumor about an affair?" Kate asked.

"It's bollocks." Jules threw out the curse self-consciously. "Charlie's the nicest, friendliest man in the world. He treats every woman like a queen, not just my mum. He's completely in love with his girlfriend, Frieda, and he brought her with him last night. The idea of Charlie hitting on my mum is just wrong."

"Can you think of anyone who would start such a rumor? Someone who had a grudge against your family?" Bhar asked, correctly sensing that Kate, taking notes again, was about to move on without exploring that angle.

"Ginny Rowland. She sat on social committees and charity boards with Mum, but Daddy was always mean to her. It was weird. Like she wasn't good enough to eat off our plates or sit on our furniture. I know she was sick of him putting her down and making her feel inferior. A few months ago, she told me Charlie might be up to something with my mum. She was wrong, and I told her so. But even though Ginny was Mum's friend, I wouldn't put it past her to spread rumors about Mum. Not if they made Daddy look like an arse."

"And Ginny Rowland was invited to the party, too?" Kate prompted.

"Yes. Her husband, Burt Rowland, was there, too. He did business with Daddy. They got on all right, I guess. Burt never says much, unless the subject is money."

"According to a constable on the scene last night, you said a party guest probably murdered your father. What made you say that?"

Jules shifted in the striped armchair, looking embarrassed. "I can't believe I said that. I went daft for a bit, I think, after I saw Daddy's body. As I ran downstairs, I saw visions of people attacking him—Charlie, Ginny, even Frieda and Burt. I kept hearing all the things he'd said to them over the years, and thinking, he finally did it, he finally went too far, and someone snapped. Daddy had a way of picking you up and flipping you onto your back—shell down—so he could dig in. A way of a finishing a row that made you never want to see him again."

Kate nodded, thinking of Malcolm Comfrey's bloodied, smashed face. "Is that how he treated Kevin?"

Jules nodded. "We were all gathered round in the front room for drinks. Daddy started on Charlie first, then Ginny. Then he set in on Kevin and just wouldn't stop. Kevin legged it, and everyone else was so embarrassed, they went home."

"What did he say about Kevin?"

"I'd rather not repeat it."

Kate paused. Remembering Hetheridge's instruction to go softly, she considered her next words with care. Then she said, "Someone may have murdered your father because of the way he behaved toward him or her. If you can tell me what he said to Kevin—to your new fiancé, at a party meant to welcome him into the family—I'll have a much better idea what your father was like."

Jules regarded Kate gratefully, like the first sympathetic face she had encountered in eons. Kate had no time to feel guilty about the manipulation—the way she had positioned Kevin's most slavish devotee to reveal his motive for murder—because the details of Malcolm Comfrey's monologue began pouring out of Jules.

"Daddy started by pretending to congratulate Kevin for being such an intelligent young man. Proposed a toast to him. Then he said he'd never heard of an artist who'd never sold a single piece, or managed to beg a grant off the socialists." Jules twisted her hands together, coloring slightly. "Daddy said he'd called Kevin's references from his portfolio, and found out he was a rotten student. And that was so unfair," Jules continued, voice rising, "because Daddy didn't bother to find out what was happening in Kevin's life at the time, or why he had trouble at school. He just soaked up a lot of wank from the instructor who hated Kevin the most, and told everyone a story about Kevin botching his *papier-mâché* project. He was sixteen years old! Then Daddy said Kevin wanted to marry a disaster like me about as much as he wanted a job in a sewer. So his hat was off to his future son-in-law, who was prepared to shovel rubbish for the rest of his life, as long as he had a wife who could grant him all the money the arts foundations had denied."

During the retelling, Jules had grown teary. Before Kate could decide what to do—actively comfort the girl, or politely pretend not to notice—the mobile phone on the coffee table emitted a hip hop tune. Eagerly, Jules snatched up the phone, squealing, "Kevin! Kevin, where are you?"

* * *

"The best part," Bhar said as he and Kate walked back to the Astra, "was when she said Kevin had a hidden side, a vulnerable side he wouldn't let anyone see. If he wouldn't let anyone see it," Bhar asked with a grin, "how did she know it was there?"

"Because it has to be there," Kate replied with a lightness she didn't quite feel. "There has to be a good side to him that loves her and appreciates her. If not, she's just a silly git, latching on to anything male to prove she can land a mate. And she's way too invested in the fantasy to start disbelieving now."

"So do you think Kevin murdered Comfrey?" Bhar asked, unlocking the passenger door for Kate. "Think the public revelation about his collapsed *papier-mâché* project sent him over the edge?"

"Won't know until I talk to him," Kate said, clicking her seat belt back into place as she inhaled new car scent again. "I'll go out on a limb and say this much. I don't think Jules did it."

"No," Bhar agreed, taking his place behind the steering wheel. "The story that she went running after Kevin to apologize for her father's behavior, and only went back to the crime scene because her mother called, is pretty convincing. Then there's statistics. Most women kill by a method that allows them to maintain a certain distance—longer than a man's reach. That means a gun, poison, even a contract hit. Taking a hot poker and beating a man to death is more of a male approach, statistically speaking."

"But Jules would cover for Kevin, if she knew or suspected he was the killer," Kate said, thinking aloud.

"Goes without saying," Bhar agreed. "What about Madge

Comfrey? Would she cover for her daughter's fiancé, if she knew he was guilty of such a violent crime?"

"I don't know," Kate said. "It might depend on her relationship to Kevin—and how happy her marriage was. Let's go see Charlie Fringate and ask him about the rumors of an affair. Then let's finally meet Mr. Kevin Whitley," she said, consulting her notes, "of 68-B, New Junction Road."

CHAPTER NINE

*C*harlie Fringate's Mayfair office was cozy and old-fashioned, with heavy antique furnishings and drapes instead of blinds. A single elderly administrative assistant sat in the reception area, behind a remarkably uncluttered desk. Her computer screen was dark, and when Kate and Bhar entered, she was reading a magazine. She glanced up at the detectives with a vague smile, as if surprised human beings had at last penetrated her sanctum.

"DS Bhar and DS Wakefield," Bhar said, showing his warrant card as Kate did the same. "New Scotland Yard. We're here to speak with Mr. Fringate."

"He's very busy," the administrative assistant murmured, with practice of one airing out a particularly threadbare lie. "Let me go and check."

A minute later, the old woman returned from the inner office. "Yes, yes, come along. He will certainly make time for the police. Bad business about Mr. Comfrey." Still muttering, she led them to Charlie Fringate's door, which featured his name in overlarge block letters engraved on a brass plate, and ushered them inside.

Fringate stood up as Kate and Bhar entered. He aimed a wide

salesman's smile at each of them. Fringate was in his early fifties, Kate guessed: a big, broad-shouldered man with a square face, superhero chin and a head full of hair so dark, it had to be colored. He was handsome in a wholesome, American-cowboy sort of way. But weighty bags drooped under each eye, and there was something in his gaze—something excessively hopeful—that made Kate wonder how many potential clients he frightened away with his naked need.

"Come in, come in," Fringate said in a hearty voice. Leaning over the desk, he shook each detective's hand before returning to his seat. He wore a burgundy-striped shirt with a matching tie and braces, the latter of which dug into his shoulders. His shirt-sleeves were rolled up to just below each elbow, as if he intended to get down to business. Or perhaps he already had, Kate thought. His desk, like his administrative assistant's, was clear of work. A large calendar-style blotter covered most of the space, scribbled over with times, names and phone numbers. His desk also offered not one but two candy dishes: a cut-crystal dish of peppermints, and a porcelain bowl of M&Ms.

"Take your pick," Charlie said, flashing his hopeful smile. "Please, sit down. Let me know how I can help. But this is just a formality, I'm sure," he added, with what Kate suspected was a habit of unwarranted optimism.

"Jules Comfrey mentioned you did business with her father. She said on one occasion, the deal went sour," Bhar began. "Can you tell us about that?"

"Sure. I did business with Malcolm on and off for almost twenty years. Used his company to ship calculators and adding machines, back in the day, before the Asians cut me to ribbons." He grinned at Bhar. "No offense. Smart people. Good at miniaturization. Most of us just couldn't compete. Now I've gone into a different line, auctioning factory surplus and what they call 'seconds'—merchandise not good enough for Mr. and Mrs. UK Consumer—and shipping it round the world. Always need the best price on global freight or the profit goes up in smoke. Malcolm and I agreed on a price for shipping a huge amount of plastics to Poland, Lithuania and the Ukraine, but just when the freight was ready, Malcolm told me his company's circumstances had changed. He increased his price by almost twenty percent. I only had an eight percent profit margin, but I was committed on several levels. So I shipped the freight, swallowed the loss and tried not to take it personally."

"Did you consider your legal options?" Bhar asked. "Since Comfrey changed the contract without notice?"

Fringate laughed. "Oh, no, it doesn't work that way. Handshake deals, that's how it's done. Never lawyers, never paperwork. And even if we did bother with a written contract, I wouldn't have turned around and sued Malcolm. Never." Fringate didn't look or sound the least bit condescending—he had an easy, pleasant way of explaining—but the unspoken meaning rang clear to Kate: people like us conduct business through gentleman's agreements. We aren't litigious, like you rabble.

"It was still a kind of betrayal. Did it make you want to kill him?" Kate asked.

Fringate gave an astonished laugh. "I really am being questioned by Scotland Yard, aren't I? Don't worry, I'm not insulted. Just doing your job, I know. Right. Did I want to kill Malcolm? No, of course not. Fact is, I wanted to ask him if he needed any help. If there was something wrong with his business, or his home life. He hadn't been himself for at least two years, especially when it came to money. And for him to change the terms of a firm deal, a deal I couldn't possibly break—that wasn't like him. I took it hard," Fringate admitted. Once again, naked need bobbed to the surface in his large brown eyes. "But no, I didn't want to kill him. Not then, and not last night. Last night was just an embarrassment, a family row. It upset that dodgy young fellow of

Jules's far more than anyone else. Frieda and I made our escape as quick as we could."

"What's Frieda's full name and address?" Kate asked. The scent of Fringate's cologne—strong and woodsy, probably sold in a plaid bottle—was making her head ache.

"Frieda Buxton. 28 Sadler, Shepherd's Bush," Fringate said. "Must you question her, too?"

"Yes. Now, can you tell us about your relationship to the Comfrey family?" Bhar asked. "Specifically, Madge Comfrey?"

Charlie Fringate's face changed. Big, open and honest, it tried to close, but only succeeded in looking wary. "I've known Madge and Jules as long as I've known Malcolm. Good people. Best sort of people."

"It's been said," Bhar said, elongating the pause, "you're having an affair with Madge Comfrey. We're not here to judge anyone's private lives. But if there's any truth to the rumor, it's much better for you to put it on the table now, rather than have us dredge it up later."

"It's not true," Fringate said. He was careful, Kate noticed, to maintain unflinching, unblinking eye contact with Bhar. "I'm a friend of Madge's. No more, no less. She isn't the sort of woman to have affairs."

Bhar did not reply. The silence stretched out for a full minute. Then Fringate, sounding all too eager to fill the silence, continued, "I really must ask who said such a thing. Gossip of that nature is just plain cruel."

"Oh, it's only gossip," Bhar said, flashing a smile. "We have to follow up on everything. Like whereabouts. After the party broke up, where did you go?"

"I drove Frieda home," Fringate said. "She was put off by the whole scene. Malcolm always frightened her a bit, with his bad temper and his way of crucifying anyone who got on his bad side. So I dropped Frieda home, went back to my townhouse and went to bed."

"Talk to anyone when you arrived home? Neighbors? A maid?" Bhar asked.

Fringate leaned back in his chair, studying Bhar first, then Kate. "I'll be boiled. You really are asking me for an alibi. My goodness. Very well. There was no one at home. No one but my cocker spaniels, whining and scraping at the door. I fed them, played with them and went to bed. I had no notion Malcolm was dead until this morning, when Madge rang me up with the news."

Bhar nodded. He started to rise, then stopped and lifted a finger, as if jogging his own memory. "One more thing. Mr. Fringate, of everyone who attended the party, you're the only one with a prior conviction. Domestic violence, 1991. Charges of stalking were also filed in 1992, but those were dropped. Care to explain?"

Fringate blew out a sigh. His expression of dismay was so genuine, and so sadly comical, Kate almost laughed. He didn't look like a man who'd been convicted of domestic violence. He looked like a man who loved his cocker spaniels.

"That conviction," Fringate said after a moment, a note of strain in his voice, "will haunt me for the rest of my life. Every time I think it's buried, it climbs out of the grave again. I assume you received the name of the person who filed those complaints."

"Helen Fringate," Bhar said.

"My wife, at the time. Our divorce was final in 1993. She even took back her maiden name. Like our marriage never existed. The 'domestic violence' was never that. I never raised a hand to her, nor would I," Fringate said with passion. "She blew it all out of proportion, and the courts decided to teach me a lesson. A life-long lesson, near as I can tell."

"What happened?" Kate asked. "We read the police statements, but it's better to hear it from you. You have to understand, a prior conviction for assault could make you a person of interest in the Malcolm Comfrey case."

"I didn't assault Helen," Fringate cried, face going red. With visible effort, he fought to regain his composure. "I was at a low point in my life. My second business had gone bankrupt. Helen announced she was leaving me. Not for another man, not because she never loved me, but because she thought I was a failure. On the night she packed up and left, I tried to stop her from getting into the taxi. That's all. I thought if I could make her stand still and listen to me, she would give me another chance."

"The complaint said you tackled her and falsely imprisoned her until the taxi drove away, and the neighbors called the police," Bhar said.

Fringate, still red, looked away. "I didn't tackle her. I got down on my knees and told her I loved her and couldn't live without her. Then I put my arms round her legs and held her so she wouldn't get into the taxi. Didn't put a mark on her. Didn't rumple a hair on her head. Just held her and told her I loved her."

"Until the police came," Kate said. She'd meant it to be a question, but it came out as a statement.

Fringate did not deny it. "The stalking business was nonsense, too. Helen was still my wife. We'd made vows. We'd shared everything for almost ten years. I was just trying to force her to listen to me. And the charges were dismissed, eventually. That time, not even Helen could succeed in turning my devotion into something sinister. And you won't be able to turn my friendship with the Comfreys into something sinister, either."

* * *

"Is he having an affair with Madge?" Kate asked Bhar, as they walked back to his Astra. It was almost noon now, and the sun felt good on her skin. Her feet, however, ached worse than ever, wedged in those cheap black pumps.

"Yes," Bhar said. "Or if he isn't, he wants to. Gave us the liar's stare. Keep looking, don't blink, don't waver, and they'll have to believe me."

"Could he have beaten Malcolm Comfrey to death? Maybe over business deals sealed with a handshake, with no legal recourse? Maybe over Madge?" Kate asked.

Bhar considered for a moment. "Yes. I think so."

"But did he?" Kate asked, turning the idea over in her mind.

"Don't know." Bhar aimed his keyless remote at the Astra, which chirruped obediently as the doors unlocked. "Let's go meet Kevin Whitley and size him up."

* * *

KEVIN WHITLEY'S address led Kate and Bhar to a council flat in a tall, charmless building that reminded Kate of one of those sci-fi flicks—the ones where the future is a landscape of white cube architecture and white polyester jumpsuits. The building's lobby was equally featureless, and fiendishly well-scrubbed. The linoleum floor was grooved by mopping, the baseboards scraped with brush marks. Even the call box showing each apartment number had been attacked with a cleaner strong enough to fade some of the tenant names. The lobby smelled overwhelmingly of bleach, and faintly beneath that, urine.

"Lovely place," Bhar said, examining the call box. "Which name are we looking for?"

"Plaster," Kate said. "Lisa Plaster is the actual tenant. Whitley just flops here. He used to live with another girl, Nan Cardwell, but Jules said they don't speak anymore. Whitley wasn't officially on the lease at Ms. Cardwell's place, either."

"Scrounger, par excellence," Bhar said, punching the call button labeled Plaster. After a moment, a female voice barked, "What?"

"New Scotland Yard. DS Bhar and DS Wakefield, by appointment," Bhar recited cheerfully into the microphone. "We're here to interview Mr. Kevin Whitley."

Silence. Then the lobby's inner doors buzzed, and they were permitted entry.

Lisa Plaster's flat was located on the eleventh floor—a long, off-white hallway where the graffiti had been washed away semi-successfully. The orange carpeting bore multiple ash burns and a deep path worn down the center. As they approached the door, Kate heard the scrabbling of a chain lock slid aside, and deadbolt turned. The door opened, and a tubby blond in a stained T-shirt and trackies faced them, hands on hips. She was about Kate's age, with a swollen nose and pink, weepy eyes.

"This is my place. Kevin's just staying here. What's he done?" Lisa asked thickly, through a cold that sealed off most of her nose. "He gave me some bollocks about being prime suspect for murder."

"I am a prime suspect for murder," called a male voice from behind her, over the sound of theatrical kicks, punches and grunts. "Jules told me I'm meant to have smashed up her pillock of a father with a fire iron. It's brilliant!"

"Mr. Whitley is a person of interest in a murder investigation," Kate said, allowing Lisa to examine her credentials. "But we're not here to make accusations. We're here to talk."

"Fine," Lisa sighed. "Have at. I need to give Benjy his bottle."

Turning away, she headed deeper into the flat. It looked like Kate's, at least in her darkest imaginings, if she ceased all housework and allowed a harsh Darwinian landscape to take shape. The orange-carpeted floor was strewn with plastic toys, a crunchy dusting of crumbs and dried beverage stains. The coffee table was piled with dirty plastic bowls, overflowing ashtrays and crumpled food wrappers.

Kevin Whitley was seated on the floor in a gamer's chair, rocking back and forth in front of the television as his fingers worked a controller. As the detectives approached, he glanced away from the screen, where two muscle-bound titans pummeled each other mercilessly, and paused the action. "Oi! Am I nicked?" He gave Kate and Bhar a self-satisfied grin.

Kevin was about Jules's age, with a high forehead, brown eyes and bleached hair sculpted into a fauxhawk. He wasn't handsome, Kate thought, nor even cute. At most, Kevin Whitley was charismatic, with an intense stare and engaging smile. Other than that, despite the pierced ears and eyebrow, he looked like a thousand other young men she might glimpse in a normal week—maybe a hundred thousand.

"I'm DS Wakefield, this is DS Bhar." Kate extended a hand.

Kevin took the hint. Giving the paused game a sorrowful glance, he stood up, wiped his hands on his jeans and shook with each detective. Sweeping aside dirty plates and chucking an action figure to the floor, he indicated the now-cleared sofa. "Take a load off."

Perching on the edge of a stained cushion, Kate said, "Your engagement party last night. I understand it was ruined by Malcolm Comfrey."

"Hey?" Whitley frowned, glancing over his shoulder to make certain Lisa was still out of earshot. "It weren't never an engagement party. Did Jules tell you that? She's always exaggerating."

Kate exchanged glances with Bhar. "That's interesting. Both Jules Comfrey and her mother described the occasion as an engagement party. One of the guests, Charlie Fringate, made reference to that, too."

"Oh, well, maybe Madge said it because she wants me in the family. She's always liked me, and I've always managed to keep her sweet. In fact," Kevin continued, giving Kate an appraising stare, "I quite like older women. They're more settled. Easier to talk to. Madge liked me from day one, and ..."

Breaking off, Whitley glanced over his shoulder again as Lisa re-entered, toddler on her hip. The boy sucked contentedly on a bottle of fizzy soda.

"You know, as far as this engagement business, Jules's family is too pushy," Kevin announced with new authority. "They know I like Ju. They know we have fun, and she's into my art. In their minds, that equals marriage. But I'm not ready to settle down. Not for one girl, much less a wife. Marriage is an institution and I'm not ready to be sent to an institution. Know what I mean, mate?" he asked Bhar.

Bhar nodded. "Sure. So—did you explain your philosophy to Jules?"

"About a hundred times," Lisa said, shifting Benjy from one hip to the other. "Let me tell you about Jules Comfrey. She's a toffee-nosed little brat who thinks she can buy herself a man. Once she called here for Kevin, and I told her to get stuffed. Kev's been trying to break it off with her for a year. If he'd just show some backbone," she grunted, her anger suddenly shifting from Jules to Kevin, "he could send the silly bint down the road."

"So you're acquainted with the Comfrey family, too?" Kate asked Lisa.

"Just by reputation, luv," Lisa said. "And that's plenty. Kev tells me everything, and I do mean everything. If he'd just take my advice once in a while, he'd be the perfect man."

Bhar turned his winning smile on Lisa. "So, just for the record. You and Mr. Whitley are ..." He trailed off, inviting her to fill the gap.

"Friends," Kevin said.

"Way more than friends," Lisa said in the same moment. Shifting Benjy to her other hip, she tried to look tough and territorial as the boy grabbed at her breast. "Whaddya think's going on here? Kev's like all men, born to stray. Don't mean he ain't smart enough to come home at the end of the day."

"That rhymes," Kevin laughed. "You're a poet, my love. Now tell me, detectives, am I nicked or not? I'm pleased as punch the old man's dead. But I'd really like to hear how I did it, since I was out with my mates all last night."

Kate took Kevin through his recollection of the previous

night, which agreed with Madge, Jules's and Charlie Fringate's accounts. The party had gone sour from the beginning. Malcolm Comfrey had warmed up by needling his other guests, then focused his attention on Kevin. Kevin had finally stormed out, gone to his favorite hangout, the Severed Head, and proceeded to crawl from pub A to pub B until passing out on the street. At dawn, he'd awakened and made his way back to Lisa's. Kate took down the names and phone numbers of six different friends, and five different pubs, all of which Kevin claimed as his alibi. It would take the junior DCs at least three days to fact-check his statement.

"What about that story Malcolm Comfrey told his guests?" Kate asked. "About an old teacher of yours, and a *papier-mâché* project?"

"That bent old scrooge Butterman." Anger flashed in Kevin's eyes. "Had to go and tell Comfrey something that happened ages ago. I was supposed to make a *papier-mâché* project for class. A burro," Kevin said. "Something mental like that. Butterman turned up over my shoulder, stumping around on his cane, and said my burro looked like a sperm whale. Bloody poofter," Kevin said. "You know what I did? I snatched that cane out of his hand and beat the whole thing to pieces. Forget *papier-mâché*. Forget burros. Forget bloody Butterman."

"Ever felt like doing something like that again?" Kate asked, holding his gaze. "Beating something to a pulp?"

"Every day," Kevin grinned. "Every bleeding day."

CHAPTER TEN

"So what have we now?" Hetheridge asked.

He was seated on the terrace of his London home, at a wrought-iron table in the center of his garden's red brick terrace. His back was to the sun, which had already passed its zenith; the position gave him an excellent view of Kate's and Bhar's faces. On Sundays, most of New Scotland Yard's crime units worked half a day or not at all, but Kate and Bhar had been keen on a face-to-face discussion. Hetheridge, who knew his mind worked best not in contemplative silence, but in the less disciplined and even raucous noise of junior detectives at debate, had agreed, and even offered to play host.

Bhar had turned up in an excellent mood, ready to dissect the case from the moment Harvey opened the door. Kate, however, had arrived subdued and unusually quiet, her mascara smudged and her blond hair twisted in an awkward knot. Even after brunch, she looked distracted. Perhaps she was overawed by the splendor of Wellegrave House? No—Hetheridge couldn't believe she spooked so easily. Dark circles lurked beneath her eyes, as if she'd missed some sleep. Surely she was preoccupied by some-thing other than the house, which Hetheridge had spent a lifetime taking for granted—the home his great-grandfather had built, and his mother had appointed with the tasteful, the classic, the impeccable. She'd loved the place. To Hetheridge, Wellegrave House was a cold, functional vessel—its best days long behind it, and probably a creaking old bore.

Like me, he caught himself thinking. He made no effort to push the thought away. He wasn't a relentless taskmaster, at least not on his subordinates. He knew they needed the rest, family time, and gentle treatment he had never required. So why did Kate look so defeated this morning?

"Start anywhere," Hetheridge said. Kate seemed to start awake, dropping her blue-flowered teacup on the saucer with a clatter.

"Right," Bhar said. "We have one violent act, assumed to have been perpetrated by a right-handed person of at least moderate strength." He glanced at his notes, open on the table. Unlike most of his contemporaries, Bhar still jotted his observations on paper, in a black leather-bound notebook. "The preliminary autopsy indicates Malcolm Comfrey died from his head wounds. His placement beside the warm fireplace made estimating time of death from core body temp woollier than usual. Still, Forensic places it between 8 p.m. at the earliest and 11 p.m. at the latest."

"Seems a spontaneous killing, rather than planned," Hetheridge said.

"Except spontaneous murders usually end in confession," Kate said, stifling a yawn. "Sorry, not bored, swear to God. Anyway, half the time, the perpetrator actually calls 999 after a spontaneous murder and vomits out exactly why he did it. The other half of the time, the escape and attempt at concealment are as spontaneous as the murder, so evidence is everywhere, and arrest soon follows."

"This murder may appear impulsive, but you make a good point. There's no subsequent trail of evidence," Hetheridge said. "Our investigators noted nothing of interest in the rubbish bins, and yesterday, Forensic agreed—the bins are clear of anything but normal household garbage. If Madge killed her husband, we would expect to find evidence on her clothes, hair and skin, or else concealed within the Comfrey house. Same with Jules. Forensic is still analyzing the house, but both women submitted to a standard post-homicide exam at Central Middlesex Hospital before relocating to their hotel. Both were declared clean."

Bhar whistled. "I've heard tarts scream for their solicitor when invited to hospital for forensic checks. Can't believe two posh birds would submit to tests without clawing out someone's eyes."

"It wasn't sold to them as a forensic rule-out," Hetheridge smiled. "It was suggested as a psychological evaluation, to ascertain whether Madge or Jules required medication or therapy after the shock of discovering Comfrey's body. Of course, once at the hospital, their clothes were taken into evidence, and the usual exams were conducted. But Madge and her daughter both signed waivers allowing the evidence to be gathered—quite possibly because they're innocent. As I said, no trace of Malcolm Comfrey's blood or tissue was found on either woman. None was discovered on their clothing, either."

"I don't like Jules as the killer, anyway," Kate said. "She doesn't strike me as tough enough to do in Daddy."

"As if not being tough enough to commit murder is a bad thing," Bhar said.

Kate laughed. "Besides, even if Jules snapped and killed her father, do you really think she has the cold, hard center to pull off what came next—concealing all the evidence, submitting to questioning and then sitting, poised, through a forensic exam?"

"Never," Bhar agreed. "But killers who seem like geniuses at first usually turn out to be nothing but lucky. Can we dare to assume the lack of evidence—current lack of evidence, anyway—is really the result of a well-executed cleanup?"

"I think we can," Hetheridge said. "Therefore: if the murder truly was spontaneous, it was a rare act of passion by an otherwise well-controlled individual. An individual who, upon returning to his or her usual mindset, could accept the enormity of the crime and move forward to conceal it, without the distractions of guilt and fear."

"Unless the murder didn't involve just one person," Kate said. "Unless it involved two people—one passionate and violent, the other cold and controlled."

Bhar sat up straighter. "Jules kills Daddy. Madge helps her conceal it."

"Or Kevin kills Comfrey, and hopelessly devoted Jules swoops in to hide the evidence," Kate suggested.

"What about Charlie Fringate?" Hetheridge said.

"Oh, he's a complete nonstarter," Bhar objected. "Approval-seeker. You could threaten to snip off his man parts and he'd lend you some good sharp scissors."

"I don't know," Kate said. "That story about clutching his estranged wife's legs until the coppers pried him off made him sound like a psycho."

"It made him sound like a wally," Bhar said. "Pitiful. Kevin's a better guess. He beat his burro with a stick."

Kate's sudden laughter was a sweet, welcome sound. Hetheridge experienced a peculiar relief as he watched her face light up.

"Sorry, sir." Kate shot him an apologetic glance. "That sounded a bit naughty."

"Off-duty, there's no need to call me 'sir,'" Hetheridge said.

"Off-duty, you'll need to call him 'Your Eminence.' But hang on," Bhar said. "What do you think of this scenario? Charlie Fringate is having a mad passionate affair with Madge. So he kills Comfrey because Madge orders him to—she wants out without the aggro of a divorce. Charlie's weak enough to do whatever Madge tells him. She masterminds the cleanup. He goes home to his doggies with the knowledge that after a suitable interval, he and Madge will marry, and he'll have Comfrey's money to shore up his current business. Which appears as likely to go bankrupt as the last two," Bhar added.

"I like that," Kate agreed, aiming a smile at Hetheridge. The deeper the discussion of the crime went, the happier she seemed. "That scenario fits everyone's characters, as I see them. But what do you think, sir—um, sorry. Anyway, what do you think? As one who—well, knows the real Madge Comfrey?"

Bhar assumed a theatrical silence. Hands clasped beneath his chin, he looked so ridiculously hopeful, like a teenage girl watching her first romantic cinema, Hetheridge couldn't help but laugh.

"Let's remember, I knew Madge twenty years ago."

"Knew her … intimately?" Bhar asked.

"Never had to beat the proverbial burro," Hetheridge said, stone-faced, as Bhar whooped with delight. "But I suppose what you're really asking is, do I think Madge is capable of murder, based on the Madge I knew years ago?" He considered the question. "No. But then, perhaps I never really knew her. Or perhaps the last twenty years have wrought an enormous change. Or perhaps the psychological premise that we are all capable of murder, given the opportunity and the right set of circumstances, is actually valid."

"I've never believed that," Bhar said.

"Me, either. Some people are weak," Kate said. "Even in a kill-or-be-killed situation, they'll curl up in a ball and give up."

"I was going to say, some people are naturally moral and decent," Bhar said. "Take my mum. Incapable of murder. Completely. My mum could never do anything deliberately cruel or immoral. It's outside her nature."

"Oh my God, you still live with your mum," Kate crowed.

"Why not? Don't you still live with the wolves that raised you?" Bhar shot back. "What's your opinion, sir? On the theory we're all capable of murder?"

"My analysis of human nature is ongoing," Hetheridge sighed. "And the data appears more complex with every passing year. There's certainly a great deal unexplored in the Comfrey murder. I'll permit you two to have your heads as far as how you investigate the following, but this is what I require. Find out if Charlie Fringate's business really is in trouble. Follow up on his assertion that Malcolm Comfrey started behaving differently about financial matters during the last two years. Look into Comfrey's will and let me know how much Madge and Jules stand to inherit. Re-interview Jules and Kevin Whitley together and try to make sense of what, precisely, their relationship is. And what about Ginny Rowland and her husband? I'm troubled that they left for the south of France on the day after the murder."

"So am I," Bhar said. "But I checked on their travel plans, and they were made four months ago. So it doesn't look like a case of fleeing the country so much as a scheduled pleasure trip. Assuming, of course, they didn't actually plan the murder four months ago. Anyhow, the Rowlands didn't pretend any distress over Comfrey's death. Didn't even ask how Madge and Jules were holding up, which I found interesting, since they're all supposed to be friends. But at least the Rowlands didn't bleat too much when I told them to cut short the vacation and return to London. They'll be back Tuesday morning. And they insist on having their solicitor present for the questioning."

"So at least we know they're not idiots," Kate said. There were nods all around.

"There's one other approach I'd like to try," Hetheridge said. "A visit to Lady Margaret Knolls. She's been immersed in London society for fifty years. She's an astute, if merciless, judge of character. I always find an afternoon with her most instructive. We'll meet her tomorrow at two o'clock, sharp."

"I've been meaning to tell you," Bhar said, "I, too, must dash to the south of France, and won't be available for any—"

"Not you," Hetheridge cut across him, turning toward Kate. "I had DS Wakefield in mind."

"Ah." Bhar leaned back in his chair, spreading his arms in a wide, satisfied stretch. "I knew there was a reason for bringing fresh blood to this team. So I can finally soak up the perks of seniority." He sprang to his feet, grinning at Hetheridge and Kate. "Fabulous brunch. I'll give my compliments to Harvey on the way out. I'd love to spend more time with you kids, but I have to go home and prepare," he concluded triumphantly, "for my date tonight."

"Congrats," Kate said. "Does she charge by the hour, or the occasion?"

"Neither. I'm hoping she'll be like you, luv—mine for a glass of Chardonnay."

"Right. Better dash home, then, and tell dear old mum which of your slacks to press."

"I am perfectly content," Bhar said, "to wear whatever Mum chooses for me. Cheers!" he called, and was gone.

"And people ask why I never had children." Hetheridge turned back to Kate. "What about you? Does a prior commitment loom?"

Kate laughed, dully this time, and shook her head, looking tired again. "No way. Right now I'm searching for a reason not to go home."

"How about a tour of the house? If you can keep from falling asleep, that is. You seem preoccupied."

"I'm not—oh, fair enough," she said. "I am. Probably look like something the cat coughed up. I was up most of the night, worried about Henry."

"Henry is ... your brother?"

"My nephew. The eight-year-old. Yesterday, his headmaster told me he's been skiving off classes and hiding in the library, making excuses to avoid the other students. Apparently he's being bullied something awful. Mostly verbal, which means there isn't a darn thing the school will do about it. They practically blame Henry for not being tough enough to stop it himself. All this time, I thought Henry was doing great. Turns out he's miserable, and doing so badly, he may fail his year and have to repeat. I always knew being Ritchie's sister was tough, but I thought being Henry's aunt was a piece of cake. I had no idea he was drowning at school," Kate said, mouth contorting as she controlled herself. "I'm useless! Some mum I'll be."

Hetheridge found himself with no idea what to say. After a moment, he settled for the truth. "You'll make one hell of a detective, though."

Kate stared. Then she wiped her eyes, sniffed and gave a high-pitched little laugh. "Would it kill you to say I am one hell of a detective? Even if it isn't quite true?"

Hetheridge smiled. "You prefer men who lie?"

When she laughed again, it was softer, and with full control. "It's all I know."

"Must be why you enjoy practicing the martial arts so much. One of the first things I noticed in your file," Hetheridge said. "You're ranked at the top of the Yard's female detectives."

"Yeah, well, they're not an athletic bunch. Eating Pop-Tarts every day and smoking between training sessions," Kate said. "I'm great at defense. I can immobilize blokes three times my size. Offense is more of a challenge. Apparently, I suffer from bad form. What about you? Bhar told me you're a champion duelist."

"Fencing," Hetheridge said. "Pastime of mine."

"I thought you were going to say passion."

Hetheridge stared back at her. He was aware of the distance between them, the drape of her shirt over her breasts, the smooth expanse of her skin. "I have no passions."

"That's it. Lie to me," Kate said. "And show me the house while you're at it. I've always wondered how a baron lives."

Hetheridge, who had never before undertaken such a working class ritual, rather enjoyed it, lingering in each room as he did his best to take Kate's mind off her nephew's troubles. He showed her the marble floor tiles imported from Italy, the Vermeer that had been prized for generations, until proved a fake, and the bedroom his great-aunt Lucy insisted was haunted. He even produced the Victorian chamber pot, still beneath the bed, where Lucy had not-so-secretly stashed a whisky bottle to fortify herself against spectral visitations. Kate was especially delighted by the antique telephone, nonfunctioning, and the antique lift, which had been reengineered to modern standards. And unlike most of Wellegrave's guests, who pretended indifference to their surroundings, since commenting upon them was hopelessly ill-bred, Kate was captivated by the lift's scarlet carpet and brass-cage door. Hetheridge was happy to oblige her with a ride.

"Let's go up to the third floor. I want to show you something."

When the bell dinged, Hetheridge pulled aside the cage-door, gesturing for her to exit first. He led her through a pair of double doors into a bright, airy room with high ceilings and a wide skylight. The walls were mirrored, and the heart-of-pine floors were bare except for exercise equipment—an elliptical trainer, a set of stainless steel weights, a treadmill and a large mat in the center of the room. The white padded mat was about two meters wide and fourteen meters long, with an electric cord running from one end to a wall socket.

"The electric *piste*," Hetheridge said. "For fencing with electri-fied swords. Less traditional but more fun."

"Will it zap me if I step on it?"

"Not at all. It would be fine for practicing hand-to-hand, if I had any aptitude for such things these days. Been many years since I was the hapless runt, getting bullied at school."

"Were you really bullied?" The worry returned to Kate's eyes, but interest flared there, too, as if she were relieved to return to the subject.

"I was indeed. My older brother was my protector until I was ten. Then he died in a boating accident. I was left alone at school, smaller than most of the boys in my year, and sad over the loss of my brother. Every day was a beating, or a long day of avoiding a beating. Finally someone suggested I take lessons in sport, after school and on weekends. I took to fencing. Needless to say, I couldn't take my *épée* to class, though heaven knows I would have. But as I learned to fence, I learned how to take hits, and give hits, and how to fall, and how to act brave when I really wasn't," Hetheridge said, wondering if he'd ever spoken to anyone in quite this way before. "By the next year, I had no more problems with bullies."

"That bears thinking about," Kate said, stepping onto the *piste* and bouncing lightly in her blue-striped trainers. "All right. You've cleverly maneuvered me into position. Come on. Attack me. Take me down."

Hetheridge glanced at his Sunday attire—crisp white shirt, tie and razor-creased slacks. "I'm hardly dressed for it."

"Come on. You mentioned my standing for a reason. Top of the women detectives, but sixteenth among both males and females. You want to prove you'd be listed higher than me, if you weren't exempt from the ranking."

"Very well." Hetheridge studied Kate, evaluating her size and posture. Then he went for her center mass, intending to pin her arms and bring her to the mat. They collided, but before he could process what was happening, his arms were behind his back, his right shoulder was on fire, and he faced the opposite wall. Kate's breath was hot against his ear.

"Oi! You're nicked," she said.

Hetheridge went still, his right shoulder still aching, as if further aggression on her part would separate tendon from bone. He shuddered, trying to shake her off. Then he began to tremble all over, his breath coming in quick, ragged gasps.

"Are you all right?" Kate diminished the strength of her grip. "I was going to make you say something like uncle, but—seriously, are you all right? Is it your heart? I—oh!"

The mat came up fast, letting out its own gasp of air as they struck, Kate first, Hetheridge on top of her. The moment her hold had lessened, he'd abandoned the heart attack routine, kicked her feet out from under her, and used her own weight to spin her around and throw her down. The impact was hard, her chin striking his chest, but he stifled a grunt of pain.

"You cheating bastard!"

"Old age and treachery will always overcome youth and skill." His hands were tight on her forearms, pinning her into place; his knees were on her thighs, his greater weight holding her down. Hetheridge meant to say more—something dry and witty had come to him as they pitched to the mat—but the words vanished, the cerebral replaced by the visceral. Her skin was warm beneath his hands; he could see her pulse throbbing in her throat. Then the wave of lust rose, filling him so fast, he almost pressed his lips to hers, almost slid his body along the length of hers.

"I ... I apologize," he muttered. Rolling off her, he got to his feet as quick as his aching left knee permitted. "I doubt I could have hurt you, but I certainly could have hurt myself, pulling a stunt like that. I don't know what I was thinking." He turned away as he spoke, pretending to fuss with his shirt and tie, hoping the physical evidence of his sudden desire would disappear before she noticed.

"Sorry I called you a cheating bastard," Kate said. He heard the mat scrape as she got to her feet. "In the heat of the moment, I forgot our relative positions."

So did I, Hetheridge thought, still amazed with himself, and wondering how soon he could get Kate on her way. *So did I.*

CHAPTER ELEVEN

$\mathcal{K}$ ate stopped by a chemist's on the way home from Wellegrave House. She bought a Diet Coke, a box of chocolate biscuits for Henry and Ritchie to share, and, after a long inner debate, a home pregnancy test. She drank the soda during the drive home, trying not to think about the pregnancy test jammed in the bottom of her bag. That could wait until morning.

When she arrived back at the flat, Henry was immersed in a book and Ritchie was positioned in front of the telly, endlessly scrolling through the onscreen guide in search of something better. Cassie, Ritchie's live-in assistant, was in the kitchen, peeling potatoes over the sink. Something fragrant, like chicken broth with rosemary, simmered on the cooker. Giving Cassie a wave and grateful smile, Kate dropped her handbag on the living room floor, retreated to her bedroom and felt a wave of sleepiness roll in like a fog. She couldn't be a zombie tomorrow. Tomorrow she had to be on. And right at that moment, there was nothing she wanted more than a long, luxurious nap before dinner.

Stripping to bra and knickers, Kate wrapped herself in her

duvet and fell asleep almost immediately. She dreamt she was working the Comfrey crime scene with Superintendent Jackson. He was snacking on powdered doughnuts, spreading white crumbly bits on the corpse's hair and shoulders.

"This murder," he pronounced, "cannot be solved without questioning the child's father."

Kate started to remind him that Jules's father was, in fact, the dead man, when Bhar, Madge Comfrey and Hetheridge appeared at her elbow. Bhar, dressed in footie PJs, clutched a battered teddy bear. Madge and Hetheridge looked embarrassed.

"The father," Jackson said, pointing at Hetheridge, who in turn pointed at Madge.

"You told me you were on the pill!"

Madge shrugged. "I don't know how our boy turned out so dark. Doesn't come from my side."

Then the scene shifted, back to Wellegrave House. They paced around the electric piste, Kate and Hetheridge, circling like panthers—she still in her bra and knickers, he in his tuxedo. Then he lunged for her. She could have deflected him, but instead let his arms go around her. He gripped her hard, so hard she fought him, his mouth pressing against hers. But then she parted her lips, letting him in, feeling the heat of his tongue, feeling herself—

Kate snapped back to reality—or perhaps reality snapped back at her, popping her across the face like a wet towel. She was in her own bedroom, a hand on her shoulder, a lanky figure looming over the bed.

"You were moaning," Ritchie said.

"Ritchie," Kate groaned—the anguished rendition of his name she emitted only when exasperated. "I've told you, don't hang over me when I sleep. Just because I move or make a sound doesn't mean you should shake me awake."

"You were squirming."

"I was sleeping!" Sweeping aside the duvet, Kate stretched,

rubbed her sticky eyes and launched herself at Ritchie. He defended himself against her tickling with flailing arms and high, girlish laughter. Soon they were both rolling on the bed, tickling and mock-slapping until Henry and Cassie, drawn by the raucous noise, arrived to choose sides in the battle. Kate was suddenly embarrassed—Ritchie might be oblivious to her state of undress, but Henry was getting much too old for auntie peep shows. Shooing everyone out, Kate got dressed. And by the time dinner was served, she'd forgotten her dream altogether.

* * *

WHEN KATE AWOKE the next morning, it was half-five. Just enough time to pull herself together and get to the Yard by seven. Heading for the bathroom, she nearly plopped onto the toilet before she remembered the pregnancy test. Retrieving the box from the depths of her handbag, she broke open the package and scanned the instructions. Then, careful not to awaken Ritchie— he'd fallen asleep in front of the telly again—she crept back to the bathroom, locked the door, and peed on the stick. Forcing herself to place it on the countertop, she brushed her teeth, showered in just five minutes and toweled off, eyeing the test. The results had developed. Two pink lines.

She blotted her hair, then picked up the test again. Definitely two pink lines. Suspecting the fluorescent light was too harsh for an accurate reading, she carried the test to the bedroom, pushing back the curtains. In the diluted early sunlight, the test looked the same: two pink lines.

Replacing the toilet lid, Kate sat down on it, naked, the test still clutched in her right hand. She felt more disbelief than shock. It wasn't true. It couldn't be true. Not from just one time, one unprotected time. The test was bad, or she'd performed it incorrectly.

Or else it was true. Her number had come up. In which case,

she couldn't dodge her responsibility: she needed to swallow her pride and call Dylan.

All her dating life, Kate had been the first to end a relationship, or else had behaved afterward as if the breakup was entirely her idea. She'd never rang a man after their final argument, never "accidentally" turned up in one of his hangouts to force a reunion, never written a soppy e-mail rhapsodizing about happier times. Certain people in this world had power over her. Certain people, by virtue of who they were, could make her plead for consideration or attention. Her bosses at the Met were a prime example. And she'd spent years, almost as long as she could remember, running after her mother, calling and searching and outright begging, especially as her sister Maura turned wilder, and Ritchie grew more and more demanding. Perhaps it was the fate of daughters, at least daughters with siblings like Ritchie and Maura, to grovel for every drop of maternal affection. But it was not her fate, Kate had long ago decided, to chase men in similar fashion. If Dylan had found a new woman, so be it. Kate would never give him the satisfaction of knowing she missed him, even a little.

But now. Now it was different, particularly if she stuck by the decision both heart and brain steered her toward. Dylan had rights. The selfish, stupid, ego-driven git had rights, if he was going to be a father.

* * *

"How many times are you going to try to call Dylan?" Henry asked. He was eating cereal, reading a book on the constellations, and listening to the telly at the same time.

Kate snapped her mobile closed. "A million billion."

"He's screening his calls. Either that, or he's turned his phone off." Henry shoveled in another mouthful of cereal. Pale and bookish, he also tended toward the chunky, and had put on a stone in the last six months.

Something else I should have noticed, Kate thought. Leaning closer, she ruffled Henry's thick brown hair. "Why aren't you wearing your glasses?"

"I can see without them," Henry said, eyes on his book.

"You can see up close. You can't see far away. You're not going to school without them."

Henry let out an aggrieved noise that reminded Kate, sharply, of Maura. "The other kids call me names. I'll blend in better without glasses."

"What do they call you?"

"Porker. Whaley McBlubber. Fart-wad-ious-maximus." Henry turned the page, then shoveled in another spoonful of flakes and milk.

"Not Four-Eyes?"

"Four-Eyed Fart Face," Henry sighed.

Kate felt two things at once. Pride in Henry, who had soldiered on with minimal complaints despite the harassment, and a thunderous, teeth-grinding rage. She wanted to go to his school and take on those little monsters herself—monsters who would surely look and sound like the same ones who had tormented her, not so long ago.

"They call me Psycho Boy, too. Psycho Boy, your mum's in a psych ward," Henry said.

"How do they know that?" Kate asked, alarmed.

"They don't. They just make up stuff—the worst stuff they can think of. They don't know in my case, it's true."

Kate thought for a moment. Then she sat down opposite him. "How would you like to learn to fight? Really fight, with a sword?"

"I wouldn't be allowed to take a sword to school. In fact, we're not supposed to fight at all," Henry said, regarding Kate as if she had lost her mind. "We're supposed to resolve things peacefully. Using our problem-solving skills."

Kate snorted. "The point isn't for you to take your sword to class. The point is for you to learn confidence. And one of the secrets of dealing with people, kiddo, is this. If they know you'll stand up to them, you won't have to actually fight them." *Not more than once or twice*, Kate amended in her head.

"I don't know." Henry stared into his cereal bowl.

"Are you kidding me? You're turning down a chance to duel like Obi-Wan Granobly?" she asked, deliberately muffing the beloved Jedi's name.

"Kenobi!" Henry roared. "Gosh, Kate, why can't you ever get it right?"

"I'll try. If you'll at least try to learn dueling."

"I won't be any good at it."

"I don't want you to be good at it. I just want you to show up for lessons. Now find your glasses and let's get you off to school."

* * *

WHEN KATE ARRIVED at Hetheridge's office, only Bhar was present, enjoying Mrs. Snell's bountiful breakfast.

"Our spiritual leader isn't here. He's been summoned to the superintendent's office." Bhar dipped his toast in egg. "Ginny Rowland and her husband want me sacked."

"Oh, Lord." Kate dropped into a chair. "Why? What have you done since yesterday, when you told them to return to London?"

Bhar grinned. "That was my crime. Telling them to return to London right away. Apparently, I owed it to such fine citizens to ask them to return at their convenience, for the complete formality of a few simple questions. They were also insulted I didn't tell them a solicitor was unnecessary. They construe that as an accusation of murder."

Kate swore a long, vicious string of oaths. Bhar looked

delighted, but Mrs. Snell, behind her desk in the outer office, cleared her throat twice.

"I want you guarding my back from now on," Bhar said.

"I'm in a filthy mood," Kate admitted. "But you were only doing your job according to SOP. How can that be a reason to sack you?"

"It isn't," Bhar said. "It's a reason for them to kick up a fuss, and try to get reimbursed for their truncated vacation. Let me tell you something about the affluent, Wakefield. They do not let go of their money easily, and they demand premium compensation for everything. It's a typical method of intimidation. Mark me—they're frightened by some aspect of the interrogation. So they're trying to put the commander on notice that they're to be treated with nothing but kid gloves, or he'll never have a moment's peace."

"Will you be taken off the case?"

"No. My money's on Hetheridge. I only bring it up as a caution to you. Learning to deal with this class of people is as much a skill as dealing with the IRA, or with American agents. I know you aren't easily intimidated, even by arseholes, but it's just as important to learn to take a certain amount of abuse without cracking. You have to keep your job uppermost in your mind when dealing with society mavens."

"Like Lady Margaret Knolls?" Kate asked, remembering she and Hetheridge had been invited for tea at two o'clock.

"Exactly. If she baits you, think twice before you rise to it. Don't let her see she can make you angry at will."

"Is that what she does to you?"

"Pretty much," Bhar admitted. "Better you than me today. I don't like to admit it, but I'm in a filthy mood, too."

"Really? How'd your big date end?"

"The way it usually does. Just me and my kung fu grip." Bhar clenched his right hand.

"Total disaster?"

"Spent the whole meal talking about her ex. How they were soul mates. How special he is. How hurt she is. How fragile her heart is right now. Didn't even get a goodnight kiss."

"But why did you ever ... hang on. Did your mum arrange that date for you?"

Bhar groaned. "Let's get off the subject."

They ate breakfast mostly in silence for the next twenty minutes, Kate's mind drifting back to the two pink lines, and the dormant mobile phone in her bag. By the time Hetheridge finally arrived, her breakfast was lodged like an anchor in her stomach.

"Fear not, the Rowlands have been placated with a season of theater tickets and a forthcoming letter of apology—from me, not you, Bhar," Hetheridge said, dropping into the chair behind his desk. "Mr. Rowland isn't particularly skilled at making demands. If I'd been dealing with his wife, I'd still be on the phone. You two will have your hands full questioning her tomorrow morning. What do you have in mind for today?"

"Jules Comfrey and Kevin Whitley together," Bhar said. "Then I'll drop Kate back by the Yard, so you two can see Lady Margaret. While you're there, I plan to spend the afternoon looking into Charlie Fringate's latest business venture."

"Excellent," Hetheridge said, massaging his right shoulder.

"Sorry if I hurt you," Kate said.

"Just old age. All my parts still work," Hetheridge said.

"Oh, yes, I couldn't help noticing that yesterday," Kate shot back. Then, with awful clarity, she realized what she'd just said. Bhar's sharp gaze went from her to Hetheridge and back again. Hetheridge stared at her, cold and blank.

"I have a great deal to do today," he said at last. "That will be all."

Kate and Bhar, comprehending the tone and stare perfectly, scrambled to depart. Once in the corridor, Bhar halted Kate, who strode toward the lifts like they alone could save her.

"Hold on. What was that about?"

"Nothing. I'll tell you later. Or never. I don't know." Taking a deep breath, Kate leaned close to Bhar's face and said, "Look. I'm having female problems. Female problems of a magnitude you can't possibly imagine. Pester me and I might go up in flames. I might even take you with me."

Bhar backed away. "Let's go question some suspects."

orking to regain her composure, Kate buckled herself into the passenger seat of Bhar's Astra while he paused outside the car to answer his mobile. When he finally got behind the wheel, he grinned at Kate, black eyes shining.

"Somebody may get nicked today. That was DC Leaman down at the lab. The neighbors situated just behind the Comfreys have a state-of-the-art CCTV system. One of their cameras captured the image of someone approaching the Comfrey house on the night of the murder, and entering through the garage. We'll have to double-check, but it sounds like the intruder was filmed in the area where you found a jimmied side door that no longer locked."

"Male or female intruder?"

"Male. Leaman just finished enhancing the image. He said the resolution is no more than fair, but still could be enough for an arrest."

"Hope he sent it to me," Kate said, producing her smart phone.

"No, he said we won't be able to make out the face on a small screen. He'll dispatch a courier with a print ASAP. We can head to the hotel and get started with Jules and Kevin's re-interview. Leaman swears the courier will meet us there before we're finished."

Kate found herself unable to sustain a conversation during the drive to the hotel, but Bhar seemed content to drive in silence, satellite radio turned off. Hoping she'd merely look eager for a follow-up call from Forensic or one of the secondary teams, Kate left her smart phone on her lap throughout the drive. It did not ring.

If Dylan continued to ignore her calls, who could help her track him down? His mother was dead, and his father, like Kate's, had disappeared early on and stayed gone. Dylan had a sister in Birmingham, but the sister's married name escaped Kate, and besides, it wasn't as if the siblings had ever been close. If this freeze-out went on much longer, she'd be forced to employ the Met's resources to locate him.

When Kate and Bhar presented themselves at the hotel room of Madge and Jules Comfrey, Madge once again opened the door.

"Good morning," she smiled. The accelerated aging of two days ago had disappeared, and Madge looked almost young, with flawless makeup, stylish attire and that stiff halo of rich brown hair. "Please come in. Jules and Kevin are waiting for you in the parlor."

Madge led Kate and Bhar to the sitting room. Jules and Kevin were snuggled on an overstuffed suede loveseat in front of the television. Jules, encased in another tight, rebellious outfit, wore indigo eye shadow and far too much eyeliner. Although the indigo made her pale blue eyes pop, the heaviness of the shade overpowered the rest of her delicate, aristocratic features. Kevin, wearing what appeared to be the same clothes he'd sported during his last interview, smelled of tobacco, pot and sour sweat. Clicking off the telly, which had been set to a music video channel, he grinned up at Kate.

"DS Walsh! I feel privileged to keep getting the hot copper. Of course, I keep getting the fecking Paki, too."

"Allah grant this infidel a terrible death," Bhar murmured, placing his hands in an attitude of prayer and bowing his head.

"Oi!" Kevin sat up straighter. "What'd you say?"

"Not Paki. Taliban. God is greatest," Bhar bowed again, still muttering. "God, remove this infidel's testicles and replace them with scorpions."

"Taliban?" Madge snapped, dark brows drawing together.

Pleased to discover the woman her chief had nearly made Baroness Hetheridge was too thick to grasp Bhar's sarcasm, Kate waved a hand dismissively.

"Kevin, tone down the racist remarks and DS Bhar will stop praying scorpions appear in your shorts. Now—we have several details to cover, so do you mind if we sit down?"

"Do," Madge said coldly.

Kate took the armchair. Bhar sat down on the brown leather hassock. Kevin, now openly hostile, stared at them, and Jules placed a protective hand on his arm. Madge continued to hover just a few paces away from the young couple.

"This interview is meant to be with Ms. Comfrey and Mr. Whitley only," Kate said. "Would you mind giving us some privacy, Mrs. Comfrey?"

Madge's eyes narrowed. "I see no reason I cannot be included. Jules and I have no secrets. Kevin is practically a member of the family. And since my husband was the victim, I certainly have a greater interest in seeing justice done than anyone here. I might also remind you," she said, "I am very well acquainted with Tony Hetheridge."

"Yes," Kate said, modulating her tone and forcing a sweet smile. "I'm aware Chief Superintendent Hetheridge called off his engagement to you some years ago, and after that, the two of you lost touch. But DS Bhar and I would never presume to discuss such a sensitive subject with you, Mrs. Comfrey. The chief will contact you himself if he considers those details significant. In the meantime, would you mind giving us some privacy with Ms. Comfrey and Mr. Whitley?"

Madge stared at Kate. "I shall speak to CS Hetheridge. And his superiors," she said at last. Then she turned away. A moment later, the suite's front door closed, not quite in a slam, but hard enough to be unmistakable.

Kate took a deep breath. "Now. Jules. When we interviewed Kevin at his current residence, a council flat shared with a Ms. Lisa Plaster, he told us he is not, in fact, engaged to you ..."

"I never!" Kevin burst out. "Why do you want to go and tell a lie like that?"

"And Ms. Plaster told us she and Kevin are, in fact, sharing an intimate relationship that continues to this day," Kate went on, cutting across Kevin's outburst. "We need to know what the precise truth is. Have you two settled on marriage?"

"Of course," Jules said. She was better equipped to verbalize her outrage than Kevin, who was reduced to shaking his head and scowling. "First of all, Lisa Plaster is a sad fat cow who couldn't pay a man to service her. Kevin's been her friend for years, but just her friend, because he would never waste himself on a loser like her. Lisa has trouble telling truth from fantasy. She's always wanted Kevin and she's never been able to accept our engagement. But we are engaged! Ask my mum! Ask Charlie and Ginny, they were at the party! The engagement's the reason my dad was such a swine that night!"

Bhar, who had flipped open his black leather notebook, read aloud: "As far as this engagement business, Jules's family is too pushy. They know I like Ju. But I'm not ready to settle down. Marriage is an institution and I'm not ready to be sent to an institution." Smiling at Kevin, Bhar flipped the notebook shut.

"I'll sue you! I know my rights!" Kevin exploded, pointing a finger at Bhar. But he did not rise, Kate noticed. Nor did he tremble with the suppressed energy that often came before an assailant attacked. Instead of leaping up and going for Bhar—taller, fitter and clearly unafraid—Kevin rounded on Jules, his eyes wide, his finger suddenly aimed at her face.

"They're stitching me up, Jules, and you'd best not believe them! I'm yours, babe, you know that. This is all balls, just hairy, slobbery balls!"

Jules looked terrified. "I know, luv, I know. I don't believe a word of it, I wouldn't ..."

"I mean, it's all your fault these wankers have climbed up my arse, innit?" Now Kevin began to shake, hands clenching into fists. "Your fault and your old man's fault. You think I need coppers beating down my door? You think I need any of this noise when I could be painting, when I could be creating my art?"

"I'm sorry. I'm so sorry." Tears started in Jules's pale eyes. "I don't believe them, I swear I don't ..."

Bhar's mobile went off. He listened for a moment, then rose and headed for the suite's entrance. Kate, left alone facing Jules and Kevin, studied the young couple, a strange ice forming in the center of her chest.

Jules, swiping at her eyes and nose, looked desperate for reassurance that she hadn't somehow angered Kevin. Kevin, on the other hand, looked puffed up again, much as he had two days before when Lisa Plaster leapt to his defense. He accepted Jules's bottomless need for his approval as his due, just as he accepted Lisa Plaster's unconditional devotion: the way a tick gorges on blood.

Sometimes I hate seeing people so clearly, Kate thought. *Sometimes I hate myself for being capable of seeing them so clearly.*

Bhar returned to the parlor in less than two minutes, a manila envelope in hand. "Kevin Whitley, New Scotland Yard has received new evidence regarding your whereabouts on the night of Malcolm Comfrey's murder." Bhar's tone was formal, but Kate recognized the gleam of pleasure in his dark eyes. "Would you care to revise your official statement on your movements and actions between seven o'clock and midnight that night?"

"What evidence?" Kevin asked, gaping at the envelope.

"A neighbor's CCTV camera took several images of you at the side entrance of the Comfrey house. This one, time-stamped ten minutes past 8 p.m., was taken just before you entered." Bhar held up two magnified, digitally enhanced photographs for Kate, Kevin and Jules to see.

Kevin Whitley stood on the threshold of the Comfrey's garage entrance, hand on the doorknob. The photo resolution was better than promised—his face was unmistakable. In the second photo, the door was open and only a shoe was visible as Kevin slipped inside the Comfrey home.

"Rubbish," Jules said, more confident now that her initial tears had passed. "And assuming it's real, how do we know it was really taken on that date, or at that time? Kevin's been coming round my house for months. Tell them, Kevin. Tell them they've got it wrong!"

Kevin had gone pale. "I want a solicitor. Won't say nothing else 'til I get one."

* * *

"Can't believe Jules Comfrey needed a sedative after we arrested Kevin," Kate told Bhar on the lift ride up to Hetheridge's office. "She certainly didn't need a sedative the night her father was murdered."

"So, given the photos, now what do you think of Kevin as the killer?"

"Still don't like him." Kate shook her head. "Malcolm Comfrey's been described as a pretty formidable personality. Did you notice how Kevin didn't dare attack you when you read back his quote? He turned his anger on the only safe outlet in the room—Jules. I know Kevin has a history of roughing up *papier-*

mâché burros, but I can't help thinking he lacks the basic nerve to physically attack a person. Or even verbally attack anyone with half a chance of striking back."

"You really don't think much of Kevin, do you?" Bhar asked. "Come on, Kate. Cut him a break. Most of us geezers aren't born with the face, body or talent of a David Beckham or a Brad Pitt. If a bloke like Kevin wants to lead a life of multiple women pleading for his attention and chasing each other out of his bed, he has nowhere to go but the bottom of the food chain. He might not be hot enough to make Angelina Jolie and Victoria Beckham beg for it, but he can drive a couple of saps like Lisa Plaster and Jules Comfrey round the bend. I'll bet when we finish investigating Kevin, we'll find two or three other hard-luck ladies in his stable. That's the real reason he hasn't told Lisa Plaster he's marrying Jules. He'd be mad to turn down Jules's money, but he's addicted to being a hot commodity. Uh-oh." Bhar laughed. "You're getting that barracuda look again."

"Sorry. Bet you think I've gone off men."

"Not at all. You really want to know what I think?" Bhar smiled. "Maybe one man treated you rather like Kevin treats Jules. Now the memory makes your blood boil."

Kate caught her breath. The lift dinged and the doors slid open, giving her an excuse to compose her thoughts. When she turned back to Bhar, she was under control again.

"I refuse to believe," she smiled, "such a gifted detective can only find a date through the efforts of his mum."

"Oh, I can scare up my own dates. But my mum has a certain type in mind for me. If I refuse to play along, it would break her heart. Ready to head back into the dragon's den?" Bhar asked, indicating Hetheridge's office at one end of the corridor.

Kate nodded.

"Care to explain what you meant about knowing all the old man's parts still work? Because the truth is probably nicer than the explanations I've concocted."

"Not really."

"Fair enough. He doesn't hold grudges. Just go in there, act professional and he'll treat you the same way he always has. Now I'm off to my research on Charlie Fringate. But second unit has promised to ring us both if Kevin drops any bombshells during interrogation." With a wave, Bhar turned and headed in the opposite direction, leaving Kate facing Hetheridge's office alone.

CHAPTER THIRTEEN

*M*rs. Snell glared at Kate as she entered the offices. "Chief Hetheridge is on a conference call at the moment. Please take a seat and—Detective Sergeant Wakefield!"

"He's expecting me," Kate tossed over her shoulder, and strode into Hetheridge's inner office without another backward glance.

Easing the door shut behind her, Kate crept to one of the chairs positioned in front of Hetheridge's wide desk. He was turned half-away from her, facing the speakerphone, but his eyes flicked toward her as he continued, midsentence: "... and when I encounter this degree of spurious complaints so early in the investigation, I begin to suspect complicity, if not an outright conspiracy."

A male voice issued from the speaker. "But both your subordinates have been perceived as offensive. And both of them, if we may speak frankly, are likely to stumble when interacting with their betters. An Indian and a disgruntled woman, isn't it, Tony? I know you've always had your idiosyncratic favorites among the detectives. But to select those two and then permit them to work unsupervised among such rarified individuals—individuals they can't possibly comprehend—is a recipe for disaster."

A female voice, vaguely familiar, as if Kate knew it from the telly: "I can't comprehend why the Indian told Mrs. Comfrey he was member of the Taliban, or why he prayed aloud to Allah prior to the questioning. If she goes to the gutter press with her complaint, it could be a nine-day's wonder."

"Madge won't go to the media," Hetheridge said, unruffled. "She threatened you with them because she knows you're terri-fied by that prospect above all others. But it's the one action she'll never take. Now if we can get back to …"

"Hang on," the male voice interrupted. "This is an anguished widow who feels mistreated during her hour of need. How can you be certain she won't air her grievances to the press?"

Hetheridge sighed audibly. Turning in his chair, he met Kate's gaze and, to her surprise, smiled. Then he swiveled back to the speakerphone. "I can be so certain because Madge Comfrey is not merely an anguished widow. Social climbers like Madge prize a certain strata of acquaintances, connections and invitations. If she, as the wife of an industrialist, embarrasses me, a peer, in the press, she will risk ostracism at a time when she might make a brilliant second marriage. She needs my good will far more than I need hers. Which is why she complained to you, George, instead of me."

The room was quiet. Then the male voice said: "I never considered the matter in quite that light."

"No. Which is why you shouldn't attempt to analyze rarified individuals you can't possibly comprehend. Leave that to me. Me and my team, who cannot be blamed for the neuroses of a few people who, not to put too fine a point on it, are all under suspi-cion of murder."

The female voice said, "I still say you should caution the Indian for that egregious reference to the Taliban."

"Consider it done," Hetheridge said.

"Is it true you've arrested Madge Comfrey's future son-in-law on the strength of two photographs?" the male voice asked, clearly struggling to find a point on which he could successfully make Hetheridge squirm.

"Photos from a CCTV camera in the neighborhood. Unimpeachable digital evidence that demands explanation. I can't allow the Yard to be accused of favoritism by skirting standard procedure, can I, George?"

"This case needs to wrap as soon as possible, Tony. I know I can trust you to further diversify your team, and put new talent on the investigation, if that's what it takes to arrest Malcolm Comfrey's killer as soon as possible."

"And successfully prosecute him," the female voice said.

"But of course." Hetheridge closed his eyes and leaned back, armchair creaking as male and female voices began to exchange perfunctory pleasantries. When the goodbyes concluded, Hetheridge opened his eyes, smiling at Kate again.

"Interesting about Kevin Whitley being seen entering the Comfrey house just before the murder. I can't say I like him as the killer."

"Me, either," Kate said.

"And please tell me why Bhar referred to himself as Taliban."

"Kevin called him an effing Paki. Bhar was living up to expectations."

"I see." Hetheridge glanced at his Rolex. "We'll need to hurry if we're to make Lady Margaret's on time. My driver's waiting in the Bentley downstairs—just let me send this e-mail before I forget."

The computer screen was positioned so Kate could see the message Hetheridge typed.

TO: deepal_bhar@met.police.uk

FROM: anthony_hetheridge@met.police.uk

Paul,

Kindly refrain from identifying yourself as Taliban when questioning suspects.

Yours,

AH

"Reprimand accomplished," Hetheridge said, rising. "Let's go."

"Can I say one thing first?" Kate asked. "Off the record?"

Hetheridge's eyes narrowed. "Proceed with caution, but yes."

"I'm sorry I spoke without thinking this morning. I didn't mean to be disrespectful. And one thing I've learned from practicing martial arts is that when men and women start grappling each other and rolling around, sometimes the men get aroused. Besides," Kate tried to stop herself, but couldn't resist concluding with a cheeky grin, "I wouldn't be much of a detective if I hadn't noticed."

Hetheridge regarded her for a moment, and then, to her relief, chuckled. "I don't know why I took such offense at your mentioning it. At my time of life, I ought to take out an announcement in the *Times*."

"The age thing again," Kate sighed. "You really have a hang-up about that, Tony." She stopped, surprised at herself, and shot him a glance. "Whoops."

"Never fear, Kate. I think we've moved beyond surnames. Now let's go."

* * *

LADY MARGARET KNOLLS'S London townhouse was not what Kate expected. She had imagined something similar to the Comfreys' home—yellow-striped wallpaper, beige window treatments, mirrors and glass. Or perhaps something akin to Wellegrave House—antique furnishings, intricate Turkish rugs, and the occasional electronic concession to modern life. So Kate was unprepared for the home into which Lady Margaret's housekeeper—a middle-aged Jamaican woman with row upon row of shiny, beaded braids—ushered them.

The foyer, painted tomato red, was lit by a black chandelier. The walls were accented with what Kate guessed were framed squares of 1970s-era kitchen wallpaper—the orange and brown geometric patterns she recalled from childhood. The housekeeper, attired in jeans and a jumper instead of a uniform, led them across a frankly fake zebra rug—it looked like someone had skinned a gigantic plush toy—and into a golden salon so gaudily opulent, Kate gasped.

Black-lacquered panels and towering Empire-style mirrors dominated the long, rectangular room. The ceiling, decorated with a mural of pinkish clouds against a dreamy blue sky, was enclosed by gilded molding. Black taper candles accented the traditional crystal chandelier. And the fresh flowers scattered throughout the room—peonies here, yellow roses there, a spray of something wild and weedy in the corner—were contained in simple plastic vases that might have come from Oxfam.

"Please make yourselves comfortable, Lord Hetheridge, Miss Wakefield," the housekeeper said, indicating a chaise longue upholstered in lime green silk. "Lady Margaret will be down shortly."

Kate perched on one end of the chaise, a pink pillow nestled against her side. "I don't suppose Lady Margaret is a drag queen?"

"No. But her favorite nephew runs a very successful design studio. He specializes in the flamboyant. Lady Margaret periodically allows him to redecorate her homes and offer them as showplaces." As he spoke, Hetheridge seated himself on a mahogany chair. Then an elderly woman appeared in the doorway, and he sprang to his feet again.

"Tony!" The woman crossed to Hetheridge, embraced him and held him out at arm's length. "Don't you look handsome! There's something different about you."

"Not that I know of," he said, turning to indicate Kate. Unsure if she should stand or remain seated, Kate stood up as Hetheridge said, "Lady Margaret Knolls, may I present Detective Sergeant Kate Wakefield, the newest member of my team."

"Now this is different," Lady Margaret said, smile fading. Like

Hetheridge, her eyes were an icy blue. They evaluated Kate with the precision of an X-ray machine, penetrating to the bone.

Lady Margaret, between seventy-five and eighty-five, was short and stocky, with none of the brittle frailty associated with old age. Her lumpy shape was somewhat concealed by her mono-chromatic linen ensemble—capri-length slacks and an oversized shirt that fluttered as she moved. Her white hair was so short and layered, it would always look the same, whether fresh out of bed or braving gale-force winds.

She was still studying Kate, her thin lips pressed together. If Lady Margaret's features had ever been pleasing, they'd settled into an androgynous mix: bulbous nose, wrinkled cheeks and cold, clear eyes.

"A woman. How progressive of you, Tony. And surprising. I always took you for a hopeless sexist."

"Haven't turned in my membership card yet. I brought DS Wakefield along to discuss the social standing of the suspects in the Malcolm Comfrey murder case."

"In other words, he comes to me for gossip. And I do my best not to disappoint," Lady Margaret told Kate. "Where is DS Bhar? Have I finally succeeded in frightening him into an alternate career path?"

"Not at all," Hetheridge said. "He was very disappointed when I chose DS Wakefield instead of him."

"I'll bet," Lady Margaret said, eyes still on Kate's face. "Your colleague DS Bhar and I got off on the wrong foot on our first meeting. I made some remarks he interpreted as offensive. He's been struggling to gain the upper hand with me ever since." She gave a small, dangerous smile. "Perhaps one day. Do you have any sensitive areas, DS Wakefield? Any topics I should avoid?"

"If I did, I'd never be fool enough to tell you about them," Kate said.

"Very wise. Let's sit. Hetty will bring in tea momentarily."

Hetheridge returned to the mahogany chair. Kate sank back

on the chaise longue while Lady Margaret pulled a gilded, pink-upholstered chair across the floor. She positioned it near the low occasional table across from Kate.

"I still don't know what to make of this salon. I feel a bit like Barbara Cartland amid all this pink and gold. My nephew, Edmund, assured me the room would provoke a reaction. And it does." Lady Margaret glanced around, pressing her lips together as if she saw the Emperor's nakedness, but found his bare bits too unappetizing to comment upon. Lifting the hem of her oversized linen shirt, she draped it across the bulge of her stomach and thighs, crossing her ankles and turning to show herself at the best possible angle.

"I once had a figure to rival yours," Lady Margaret told Kate. "Bosoms and backsides were all the rage then, thank God. Now with this Posh Spice creature running amok, the style is less like a woman's shape and more like a stick insect." She looked at Hetheridge. "I assume you'd like to know what your old amour, Madge Comfrey, has been up to since you so caddishly left her at the emotional altar?"

Hetheridge flicked his tie into place and lifted his chin slightly —gestures Kate now recognized as signs he was fully engaged in a conversation, no matter how neutral he appeared.

"That would be very helpful. Some of it is a matter of public record, of course. Madge married Malcolm Comfrey just two months after we called off our engagement. There was talk at the time that I'd caught her cheating with Comfrey, but it wasn't true. I never met the man—or if I ever did, it was in passing at some event or another, and I failed to register who he was."

"Madge was pilloried for her whirlwind romance with Comfrey," Lady Margaret said. "Mind you, she did well to marry him, financially speaking. She was quite the up-and-comer when she nabbed you, Tony. Considering she came from a third-rate family and had no real connections of her own, landing a baron was a coup. When you rejected her—and yes, I know you never meant for the decision to be publicly recognized as yours rather than hers, but these juicy details always get out—Madge was ruined for the titled marriage market. Since you were finally on track to do your duty to the family name," Margaret continued, smiling at Hetheridge, "by choosing an appropriate wife of acceptable stock in her childbearing years, it was widely assumed, in the best misogynistic tradition, that you dropped Madge after discovering something unsavory about her."

Turning to Kate, Lady Margaret went on, "You must understand, my dear Kate—may I call you Kate?—that Tony's choice of a dirty, embarrassing career in the Met, of all things, humiliated his parents and made him a laughingstock. Something gave him the courage of his convictions to buck his social set and choose a highly eccentric path. So when he announced his engagement to Madge, there was a general feeling that blood and breeding had prevailed at last."

"And what did you think," Hetheridge asked, "when I planned to marry Madge?"

"I thought you'd taken leave of your senses," Lady Margaret said.

"Why?" Kate asked.

"Because Madge was, and is, a gold digger. She wanted Tony for his money and title alone. Her low connections and reputation for sleeping around, I could overlook. Her latching onto my dear friend as the quickest means to a privileged life, I could never condone. Oh, here's tea. Thank you, Hetty."

Nodding, the Jamaican housekeeper placed the silver tray on the low table and withdrew. Lady Margaret picked up the teapot—also silver but of sleek modern design—and poured tea into three cups.

"Try the lemon ones," she advised Kate, indicating a three-tiered server crammed with biscuits and teacakes. "At any rate, I consider myself a good judge of character, and I can't imagine

Madge murdering her husband over something as pedestrian as a reasonably discreet affair."

"You mean between Madge and Charlie Fringate?" Kate asked.

"No." Using silver tongs, Lady Margaret extracted one sugar cube from the bowl and dropped it into her tea. "You know, I wondered about them," she continued, smiling at Kate. "But you're the first person I've heard suggest such a thing. So if Madge and Charlie are having an affair, it's better than discreet. It's clandestine."

"Then what affair did you refer to?" Hetheridge asked.

"Why, Malcolm Comfrey and Ginny Rowland, of course," Lady Margaret said.

CHAPTER FOURTEEN

"*T*hat's interesting," Hetheridge said, glancing at Kate. "Jules Comfrey seemed convinced Ginny Rowland despised her father."

"Ah, well, love and hate, and the ever-shifting line in between." Lady Margaret sipped her tea. "I understand Malcolm and Ginny were once powerfully attracted to one another. But such things wane. After a year or so, Malcolm lost interest, and Ginny found Burt Rowland. Burt always struck me as a bit of a dullard, not to mention a cold fish, but who knows what goes on behind closed doors? Never figured Burt for the sort to marry a, how shall I put it—career girl?"

Hetheridge leaned forward, taking Lady Margaret's meaning at once. Kate, too, made the leap.

"Ginny Rowland was on the game?"

"Just the phrase I was looking for," Lady Margaret said, delighted. "You sound like my nephew Frederick. He watches a great many crime dramas."

Kate glanced at Hetheridge. "I'm assuming neither Malcolm Comfrey nor Burt Rowland were the sort of blokes to pick up girls off a curb. Did Ginny Rowland work out of her own flat, or was she part of some posh escort service?"

Lady Margaret beamed at her. "I wish I knew. Fascinating to learn of such things. And mind you, I'm not suggesting Ginny Rowland broke any laws. Frederick has assured me that prostitutes who operate from home are quite legal."

"One girl, working alone in her own space, is an entrepreneur," Hetheridge agreed. "Two girls or more makes it a brothel, and thus illegal. We'll certainly look into Ginny Rowland's background."

"Why, Tony, I had no idea you were so involved in the enforcement of morals and good behavior."

"I'm not. That sort of thing falls to other units. But on the night Malcolm Comfrey was murdered, didn't Jules claim her father treated Ginny Rowland like a cheap whore?" Hetheridge asked Kate.

Kate reached for her bag, searching for her smart phone and the wealth of notes it contained, and then stopped, smiling at him. "You're right. I'm sure that phrase is in my notes. Quite a memory you have there."

"For an old man," Hetheridge said.

"Hah," Lady Margaret burst out. She did not look amused.

"Ginny Rowland seems to have propelled herself right up the social ladder," Kate said. "Protecting a secret that would make her and her husband social pariahs is as good a motive for murder as any."

Hetheridge nodded. "You and DS Bhar may find tomorrow morning's interview quite fruitful. I don't suppose you have any more surprises for us, Margaret? Any nuggets about Jules Comfrey? Or her fiancé Kevin Whitley, whom we currently have in custody for breaking into the Comfrey house on the night of the murder?"

"Jules Comfrey?" Lady Margaret dismissed her with a flick of a hand. "Tedious girl. Verging on the nonentity. I despise this generation who enters adulthood with no idea of who they are, or what they want to be, flailing around for the next ten years like a fish in a blender. If I'd been given access to the possibilities modern nineteen-year-old females take for granted, I would have lived a remarkable life indeed. As for her fiancé, I never met him. But I imagine he has a great deal of explaining to do. Can't you confront him with fingerprints, or DNA, or something like that?"

"It's in the works," Hetheridge said. "Forensic Services is over-burdened at present, but we may have a complete report by tomorrow, or the next day."

"More than one house on fire, eh, Tony?" Lady Margaret said. "I wonder you haven't moved up to commander by now."

"Veteran of the public schools though I am," Hetheridge said, "there's only so much institutionalized buggery even I will submit to. Chief superintendent is as far as I will likely ever rise."

"Commander would be more fitting for a man of your talents," Lady Margaret said. "Less dangerous. That incident where you were nearly killed on that miscreant's doorstep comes to mind."

Startled, Hetheridge shot Lady Margaret a cool, repressive glance. She gazed back at him, eyes sparkling with strange mischief.

"I heard about that before I was even assigned to the chief," Kate said. "Legend has it he never flinched. Could have repelled the bullet with his stiff upper lip. And didn't miss even a day's work after the experience."

Still more surprised, Hetheridge was grateful for his lifelong tendency to assume a poker face when ambushed. Instead of coloring or stammering, he said, "Ancient history." Taking a sip of his now-cold tea, he replaced the cup on its saucer and smoothed his tie back into place. "We're grateful for your time, Margaret. Now I believe we must return to work."

"Indeed." Lady Margaret held his gaze, that mischievous glint still in her eyes. She was communicating something to him, something he was too thick or self-absorbed to receive. Then, with a half-audible sigh, Margaret turned back to Kate with a smile.

"I wish I could be a fly on the wall when you interview Ginny and Burt tomorrow. Burt comes from a family with pretensions that would make the royal family look common. And Ginny long ago shed any signs of her entrepreneurial past. Don't wear anything like you have on now, my dear, or they'll eat you alive."

Kate glanced at the suit she wore—the gray-pinstriped number, pink shot through the weave, and black lace accents. Hetheridge remembered it from her first day in his office. He was no judge of women's fashions, but he recognized bargain fabric and substandard tailoring when he saw it. Kate's choice to accessorize the suit with sheer black hosiery and shiny black pumps —"do-me pumps," as Superintendent Jackson and others around the Yard called them—changed the suit's original message, which was "shop girl on a budget." The new message, as Mrs. Snell put it, was "tart subpoenaed into court."

"What's wrong with this suit?" Kate asked. Hetheridge had no intention of intervening, but he was glad she didn't sound angry.

"It's cheap. Cheap and silly," Lady Margaret said. "Lace is for knickers. You should invest in well-tailored suits that complement your figure rather than squeeze for dear life across the hips and bosom. Black hosiery is out altogether. It's bare legs now, or if the Met won't allow it, sheerest nudes no one will see. Your shoes should be stylish but sensible. No more pointed toes and no teetering heels. Take the time to find classic pieces, pieces that are above reproach, yet do not draw attention to themselves. A professional woman at your level should be noticed only for herself, not for the distraction of her sartorial choices."

"Thank you, Lady Margaret. That's food for thought." Serene and composed, Kate glanced at Hetheridge, who nodded. They rose to take their leave.

Lady Margaret also rose. She moved closer to Kate to deliver her parting remarks.

"If I might be so bold, I suggest rethinking your hair, too. It's rather blowsy and wild, isn't it? Like you comb it once in the morning and let it muddle through the rest of the day as best it can. Perhaps a shoulder-length cut? Maybe even a chin-length bob. That and a can of hairspray—and a mirror, if I'm honest— would do wonders for your presentation."

"Of course. Thanks again," Kate said, accepting Lady Margaret's hands in a warm clasp. Before she could say more, her smart phone rang from her bag's innards. Looking relieved, Kate turned back to Hetheridge.

"I'm sorry, but I'm expecting an important call. May I...?"

"Go right ahead. I'll say our goodbyes."

When the front door closed behind Kate, Lady Margaret turned to Hetheridge.

"I like her, Tony. As much as I like Paul Bhar, as a matter of fact. And I see you like her, too."

"I wouldn't have chosen her for my team if I despised her," Hetheridge said, unnerved, as always, by Lady Margaret's powers of perception.

She snorted. "Have I become infirm? Feeble? You can't puff and prevaricate with me. I won't have it. And I daresay I know what's different about you."

"I don't know what you mean."

Lady Margaret scowled. "I hope that's a lie. I adore you, Tony. I always have. But you can't be a fool your whole life."

* * *

KATE WAS LEANING against the Bentley when Hetheridge emerged from Lady Margaret's townhouse, directly into the glare of the late afternoon sun. Shielding his eyes, he crossed to Kate, who was idly slapping her mobile against her thigh.

"Bad phone call?"

"Telemarketer. I should have looked before I dashed off to answer. And you should get some sunglasses," Kate added. "You're always peeking out from beneath your hand."

Before Hetheridge could reply, Kate dove into her bag, coming up with several wrong items before producing a pair of black-lensed tortoiseshell sunglasses. "These are Ritchie's. I carry them around because he always forgets, then starts whining. Try them on."

Obliging her, Hetheridge did so, and was immediately more comfortable. Using the Bentley's side mirror, he studied his reflection, still worried he looked ridiculous, like a grandfather out to recapture his youth.

"You look fine." Kate sounded amused. "Not that you'll trust my fashion choices. But you can always venture inside and see if Lady Margaret approves."

"Your opinion is good enough for me. Well done, by the way. You stood up to her critique without losing your composure. You did far better than Paul on his first foray into her lair."

"He warned me," Kate said. "And really, from what he said, I expected worse."

Hetheridge regarded Kate silently. He considered himself a good judge of when his subordinates were putting on a show of professional bravery, and when they were truly unshaken. Kate's serenity seemed genuine.

"You really weren't offended, were you?"

Kate shook her head. "Grow up where I did, with your mum on the game, a schizophrenic sister and a mentally retarded little brother, and believe me—you build up a tolerance to unsolicited opinions. But you looked a little aggravated, Chief. When she mentioned your famous brush with death."

"Ah. Then my poker face isn't what it used to be." Hetheridge told himself to open the Bentley's door and usher Kate inside. Instead, he said, "Margaret is one of the few people who knows how difficult that incident was for me. Why she chose to bring it up over tea, while we were discussing something entirely different, I can't imagine."

"So the story about you staring down the gunman with your fierce glare isn't true?"

"No. It was the single most terrifying moment of my life. And I didn't go right back to work. I had a bit of a breakdown. Considered early retirement. Contemplated holing up in the country, where I'd never risk another gun in my face again."

"It changed you?"

"No. It could have changed me. But I refused to let it. At the time, I thought I'd won a battle inside myself. Now ..." Hetheridge found himself again speaking unguardedly to Kate, as he had at Wellegrave House. "Now I'm not sure if I didn't turn my back on an experience that was meant to change me."

"And nothing like that ever happened since?"

"Once." Something about Kate's interest, and his own openness, finally sounded alarm bells in Hetheridge's skull. He had to divert this conversation away from himself, quickly. "So what of Lady Margaret's fashion advice? Do you plan on taking it?"

"Think I should?"

"As a matter of policy, I never give women advice on clothing or accessories." Hetheridge opened the Bentley's door for her, but as she climbed in, couldn't resist adding, "Except this once. Don't cut your hair. She was dead wrong about that."

CHAPTER FIFTEEN

Ginny and Burt Rowland, apparently not pacified by their complimentary theater tickets and forthcoming letter of apology from New Scotland Yard, managed to miss their flight from France, postponing the interview another day. So Tuesday morning passed uneventfully, with Bhar offering confirmation that Charlie Fringate's current business was perhaps six months from insolvency. In the interview room, Kevin Whitley offered nothing of substance. After a long conference with his solicitor—a top-drawer litigator retained by Madge and Jules Comfrey—Kevin changed his original story, that the CC camera photo was misdated or a nefarious digital fabrication, to something simpler.

"I forgot my phone. Went back to get it," he told Kate and Bhar. "Knew the door was busted and got in that way. Then I met my mates at the Severed Head pub. No crime there." He looked pasty, thin and frightened as he spoke. The cocksure ladykiller had changed into a mousy boy.

"By the way—sorry I called you an effing Paki, mate." Kevin eyed Bhar hopefully. "Racist, innit? Didn't mean nothing. Can you tell me how much longer I'll be in here?"

Not much longer, Kate thought, although she and Bhar concluded the interview without ever tipping off Kevin how close his release might be. Forensic Services had confirmed Kevin Whitley's fingerprints were not on the murder weapon. It had, in fact, been wiped clean, and bore no prints at all. Malcolm Comfrey's study had contained a mélange of prints: Madge and Jules Comfrey, Charlie Fringate, Burt Rowland, and even—interestingly—Ginny Rowland. Of course, Ginny and Burt Rowland considered being forced to provide fingerprints for electronic transfer from France another outrageous insult, but they had grudgingly complied. Only one partial print belonging to Kevin Whitley had been found, and that was on the doorjamb. The print's location was several meters from the corpse—hardly the sort of compelling evidence that might lead a judge to deny bond.

"The fact that Kevin has no priors makes it even harder," Bhar said. "It's also difficult to argue he's a flight risk when the victim's family members are his biggest supporters."

"I don't suppose you learned anything new on Ginny?" Kate asked.

"No. I hoped the fingerprints might turn up a prostitution arrest under her former name, Ginny Castle, but there's nothing. She either worked alone within the limits of the law, or else one of her previous employers—all of which look legit at first pass—was a deep-cover escort service to the wealthy and privileged. I'm still digging into that possibility. Might ask the old man to call up a few of the companies, ask for female companionship, and see if he gets any bites."

Kate giggled. "You wouldn't dare."

"How little you know me. It's always been a dream of mine to witness His Lordship soliciting hot, illicit sex. Are you heading home?" Bhar asked the question in a way that implied no criticism—rare among Kate's peers, who often measured their career worthiness by how rarely they departed before 7 p.m.

"Afraid so. Got an appointment," Kate called over her shoulder. Glancing at her watch, she wondered how long it would take her to get to Harrods Knightsbridge.

* * *

THE COMPLIMENTARY SERVICES of the personal shopper took five hours—four hours and fifteen minutes longer than Kate, in her innocence, had budgeted for herself. She'd been measured, fitted, re-fitted, quizzed about the minutiae of her work life, and led to pinpoint preferences she'd never known she had. Did she like earth tones or power colors? Did she value clean, elegant lines, or prefer the edgy and up-to-the-minute? Did designer labels matter, or only fabric and cut? Were cuffs or pleats strongly objectionable? What about scent, shoes and the eternal debate— silver or gold?

Famished and suffering from sensory overload, Kate retreated to the Green Man Pub on the department store's ground level. At home in the smoky, old-fashioned pub atmosphere—a fabrica- tion, of course, but a loving one—Kate ordered a roast beef sand- wich, chips and a beer. Then she was forced to ask the waitress to replace the beer with cola when she recalled, still with that sense of unreality, that pregnant women were supposed to avoid alco- hol. Even without a beer, the late lunch did the trick. After a half hour in hiding, Kate forced herself to climb via escalator back up to the brightly lit world of the personal shoppers, to view what they'd assembled for her.

Six suits were the foundation of her new work wardrobe— black, chestnut, gray heather and navy pinstripe. Each suit was silk, and accompanied by both slacks and skirts. They fitted beautifully—so beautifully, in fact, Kate decided to confide her pregnancy to the personal shoppers. The skirts, she learned, could easily be adjusted, and Harrods would be happy to provide tailoring to accommodate her changing figure. The other acces- sories, including modest leather shoes that looked grandmotherly, but won Kate over with their cloud-like support, would carry her through the nine months just fine.

"Career women don't drape themselves in sacks anymore, just because baby's on the way," a cheerful assistant told Kate. "These days, you make fashion fit you, and display your bump with pride."

Not quite convinced, Kate consigned that image of herself—the same, except for a beach ball of a belly, knocking over evidence as she examined crime scenes—to the recesses of her mind. She probably had two or three more months to enjoy her new clothes before the jig was up. And although she didn't consider herself a clothes person, she had to admit, it was fun to let a team of professionals fuss over her until they got it right.

"I realize this is a substantial outlay," the saleswoman continued, presenting Kate with the bill. "But you'll never regret investing in yourself."

She's not sure I can pay for all this, Kate thought, handing over her debit card. She wished Henry, who often accused her of meanness, could see her release her grip on so many pounds. She scrimped on rent, her car, groceries and—until now—her wardrobe. She never revealed to any lover, including Dylan, precisely how much she earned, or how much she saved. Ever since she assumed responsibility for Ritchie, including the hiring of Cassie—a necessity partially subsidized by government agencies, thank goodness—Kate had guarded her finances. She had a fair idea what Ritchie's lifetime care would cost, and she meant to be ready.

But this really is an investment, Kate told herself. *If I look more professional, I'll get better assignments and quicker promotions. And that means more money for Ritchie, for Henry and for Baby Whatsit, too.*

Trailed by a team of smiling salespeople carrying Harrods bags, Kate stowed the entire purchase in her car's boot, grateful for the experience and relieved to escape it. Perhaps it was a sad commentary on her as a person, but when she missed work, she really missed it. And before she returned home to Henry, Ritchie and whatever amazing dinner Cassie was preparing, shouldn't she drop back by the Yard and make sure she hadn't missed any new developments?

The offices had mostly cleared out. The lifts were blessedly swift, and the only sound was of vacuums and floor-polishing equipment as the cleaning staff tackled another day's filth. When Kate arrived in Hetheridge's office, she found Mrs. Snell still at her desk, typing with demonic speed.

"Good evening, Sergeant," Mrs. Snell said, barely glancing at Kate. "I thought you'd taken a vacation day." Her tone contained all the censure Bhar's earlier question had omitted.

"That's right. Just dropped an obscene amount of money at Harrods. Can't spend every night here, hunched over my computer, or I'll end up a mad old bat without a life. Looks like Tony's in his office. I'll let myself in."

Kate entered quietly, in case Hetheridge was on another conference call, or in the midst of something private. Instead, she found him sans jacket, tie loosened, leaning back in his executive chair with his eyes closed. He looked like a man who had stayed too late at work, and fallen asleep.

Kate continued to clutch the door handle, wondering if she should go back the way she came. As she leaned against the door, indecisive—and not relishing the prospect of re-engaging Mrs. Snell so soon—the door creaked, and Hetheridge opened his eyes.

"Kate. I thought you went home hours ago."

"I did. Sleep in here often?" She took a seat in front of his desk.

"I wasn't sleeping. Thinking. Best time to do it, when most people have gone. There's little chance of phone calls and e-mails and drop-in visits interrupting me."

"It looked like sleeping," Kate said, smiling. "Did I miss

anything?"

"Bhar found a possible lead in one of Ginny Rowland's former employers, Venture Perfect Temporary Services. It's almost certainly a front for an escort service catering to the sort of men who would never go curb-crawling, or risk a walk-up. I'd like the two of you to ask Mrs. Rowland about it tomorrow."

"Of course. Did Bhar tell you Kevin's stonewalling us?"

"That's to be expected. If he'd really returned for something as simple as his phone, he would have said so at once. Yet I still find it difficult to imagine him as the killer whom Malcolm Comfrey allowed to stir up the fire in front of him. I also have trouble seeing Kevin wiping down the murder weapon while it protruded from Comfrey's eye socket. Again, we return to someone with considerable self-control."

"So why did Kevin return to the house? It couldn't have been to talk to Jules. He ignored her calls all night."

"My first guess would be drugs. Perhaps he left his stash in the Comfrey house, and didn't want to go the night without it?"

Kate raised her eyebrows. "Interesting. But based on what?"

Hetheridge laughed. "Years and years of investigating suspects like Kevin Whitley. Also his arrest toxicology report, which was positive for marijuana and heroin."

"That could be why he looked so deflated today. He may be having trouble finding gear in lockup."

"Whereas if he enters Her Majesty's prison system, he'll have no trouble at all. By the way, there's one other development," Hetheridge said. "An eyewitness has come forward—Patsy Mather, the Comfreys' neighbor the next street over, where the Comfreys' back lawn abuts Mrs. Mather's back lawn. She says she waited this long because she felt disloyal to her neighbor— which I take to mean, her class—by speaking to the police. But when she read we'd arrested a male, she decided to tell us she saw a woman exit the Comfrey house around half-nine or 10 p.m., on the night of the murder."

"Did Ms. Mather give a description?" Kate asked, excited.

"Not really. Dark hair, which sounds more like Madge and Ginny Rowland than Jules, who might look blond from that distance, even with the security lights. Ms. Mather saw a female exit the back door, walk out of the lit area and re-enter the house about five minutes later. She was carrying something small in both hands when she exited the house, but returned empty-handed. Ms. Mather thought it was odd, but not remarkable, not until the police lights and sirens gathered around the Comfrey house. I think …" Hetheridge broke off as Kate's mobile rang inside her bag.

Sighing, Kate thrust a hand into the bag, coming up with the phone on her first attempt for once. The blue screen indicating the phone number, unfamiliar to Kate, began with 0121, which meant it came from Birmingham.

"Sorry," she said to Hetheridge, and put the phone to her ear. "Hello?"

The woman on the other end asked Kate her name, gave hers, and then said something incomprehensible. The tiny hairs on the back of Kate's neck rose, and her stomach went cold, although she never remembered those sensations later.

"What? What did you say?" Kate demanded, raising her voice, as if the caller were hard of hearing instead of speaking words impossible to process. Those words issued into her ear again, faster now—frustrated, demanding, surreal.

"I don't—you can't—no!" Kate said, or meant to say, but it came out as a scream. Before she knew what happened, she'd screamed again, an ugly sound like a snared animal. Then Hetheridge was there, Mrs. Snell was there, and her phone was on the floor, barely visible through the distortion of tears.

"What is it?" Hetheridge's arm went around her shoulders.

"Dylan," Kate breathed, sure she was dreaming. She must have been dreaming, because nothing else made sense. "He's dead."

CHAPTER SIXTEEN

*K*ate clenched her hands in her lap, still fighting dry heaves, which threatened to start again at any moment. She felt cold despite Hetheridge's jacket over her shoulders, and when he opened the Bentley's door and led her out into a cavernous parking garage, Kate blinked at the familiar sight and nearly burst into tears.

"This shan't take long," Hetheridge said in her ear. His voice steadied her—it was real, and strong, and made her believe some strength still resided in her, too. "It's the last thing you can do for him. Then he'll be at peace."

Kate nodded, allowing herself to be led toward the garage's lifts. Dylan's sister Barb had explained the situation to Hetheridge, who'd jotted down details as Kate rushed to a toilet to heave up her pub grub. A South London bobby had found Dylan in an alley fifteen days before, curled in a fetal position behind some rubbish bins. His throat was cut, his wallet and phone were gone, and there was nothing on his person to identify him. After forty-eight hours on a steel gurney, no one had called a police station or hospital searching for a man of his description, so the bureaucratic wheels of identifying an unclaimed corpse began to turn.

They would have run his fingerprints, Kate knew. He had no criminal record, so that was a dead end. Then they would have taken dental pictures and sent them to a lab. The lab would have made inquiries with London dentists, and when they found a likely match in Dylan, they searched for a blood relative. They found Barb in Birmingham and asked her to positively identify the body.

But she couldn't come to London, not with three kids and a husband always on the road, Kate realized. *So she called me.*

Steered by Hetheridge, Kate found herself in the morgue's sub-basement, where unidentified bodies, corpses ruled to be police evidence, and cadavers quarantined for infectious disease were kept. This section of the morgue, unlike the more modern facility the next floor up, looked very much like the morgue seen in countless TV programs and movies—beige walls, merciless fluorescent lighting and steel drawers in the walls, designed for long-term storage. Dylan, who'd considered the word "normal" an insult, might have been pleased to know his earthly remains had taken this odd detour between expiration and interment.

"Just think. Malcolm Comfrey's in one of these drawers," Kate said. The words came out high-pitched, giddy. The coroner on duty, a tall man with bad teeth, studied her like he might study a new arrival.

"No, he's not," Hetheridge said. "Forensic Services released Comfrey for burial yesterday after the autopsy report was filed. The affluent are always fast-tracked, even in death." He put a hand on Kate's forearm. "Are you ready for this? We can return in a quarter-hour, if you wish."

Kate shook her head. Her nostrils stung with the heavy odor of antiseptic. "I want to see him. I have to see him."

"Dylan Corrigan, as the decedent's now presumed, in number eighteen," the coroner said, consulting a computer printout on his clipboard. Glancing at Kate, he attempted to assume some expression that did not come naturally to him—empathy, perhaps—and succeeded only in looking tired. "I should warn you, number e—Mr. Corrigan, as presumed, bled out at the scene and was discovered two to four hours post-mortem. The city recommends unidentified persons be kept at optimum refrigeration, and we complied. However, restorative work will still be needed if you desire an open casket service. You may find the deceased's appearance upsetting, and you may detect an odor."

Throat closed, Kate found herself unable to do more than nod. Hetheridge's grip on her tightened, and he helped her move forward as the coroner unlocked drawer eighteen and slid it open. He gave Kate a moment to take in the man's shape beneath the green sheet, then drew it back, exposing the corpse's face.

It was Dylan. He looked exactly as Kate, given her experience, had imagined. His face was sunken and blue, the bones hideously prominent, lips bluish-black. There was an odd bulge around his ears and hairline, as if his remaining blood had settled as he waited within that refrigerated drawer.

"It's him." Kate stiffened under Hetheridge's grip, pulling away. "Excuse me. I need the toilet," she said, and escaped as fast as her wobbly legs could carry her.

* * *

"I don't want tea." Kate knew she should at least attempt to sound grateful. "I'll just puke it up."

"Brandy, then," Hetheridge said, maneuvering Kate toward the sofa in his dark-paneled study. "I have a liquor cart right here. Cognac, I think, unless you prefer sherry."

"Neither. I can't drink anything."

Ignoring that, Hetheridge removed two cut-crystal glasses from the cart's second shelf, then selected a decanter from the spirits crowding the top shelf. He removed the stopper, filled each glass a quarter full, and brought the drinks to the coffee table. Kate stared at hers, but did not move toward it. Hetheridge started to sit beside her, then seemed to think better of it, choosing the leather wingback opposite her instead.

The silence stretched out, infinite. Kate had no desire to fill it. Finally, Hetheridge took a sip of his cognac and spoke.

"Tell me about Dylan. I presume he was your lover."

Kate nodded. Someone—that manservant Harvey, she guessed—had made up the fire, which was actual wood instead of gas or electric. It crackled merrily, providing the study's only light, except for one brass lamp behind the sofa. The study was so warm and cozy, like a family's retreat on a picturesque Christmas Eve, Kate again felt swallowed by the surreal. Was she really sitting in Lord Hetheridge's London townhouse at midnight, being quizzed on her sex life?

"He was. We spent the last two or three months breaking up and getting back together," she said. "Then we had the big breakup, and he stormed out. Came back an hour later for most of his stuff, and I never saw him again. That was three weeks ago."

"I suppose that's why his death went undiscovered for so long."

"I thought he had another girlfriend. That he'd just legged it out of my life. If I'd known he'd really disappeared, if I'd thought there was any chance he was hurt or in trouble ..." Kate broke off, reining in her emotions. The effort was suffocating.

"I'm sure he knew you cared for him," Hetheridge said.

Kate blinked away fresh tears. "No, I didn't. Not at the end. Maybe not ever. He was just another of the same type—handsome. Clever. And bone idle. But when I found out, I assumed he'd be there for me. I assumed he'd help, and it would make a better man out of him. I never imagined this. Every time ..." Her voice broke, and then she was helpless in the grip of hard, humiliating sobs. "Every time I think someone will stand by me, every time I think they'll stick around, they disappear. I hate it," she said thickly. "And I hate him, the stupid bastard! He was only thirty-two! How can he be dead?"

"It just happens. Most of the time, it doesn't make sense. But what do you mean, when you found out, you assumed he'd help?"

"With the baby!" Kate cried, and broke into fresh sobs. These carried on until she had to choose between breathing and weeping. Then she began to calm herself, forcing in long, deep breaths.

"I'm pregnant. It was an accident," she added, as if Hetheridge couldn't guess.

"Sometimes that just happens, too."

He didn't sound embarrassed. But when Kate looked at him, some quality in his eyes told her the revelation made him uncomfortable.

She didn't know what to say. Neither, judging by his silence, did Hetheridge. Only the fire interrupted the stillness, flames leaping higher as the logs split. At last, able to bear it no longer, Kate made her way to the loo. There she blew her nose, washed her face, and patted it dry. The towels on the rack were soft and pure white—miles away from the towels Henry and Ritchie routinely ravaged.

Decent of the chief to take charge during my moment of weakness, Kate thought. His consideration went beyond anything she expected from a superior officer—or from anyone, come to that. She needed to thank him, apologize for her innumerable professional lapses, and leave him in peace.

When Kate returned to the study, Hetheridge was in the chair beside the hearth. Taking an iron from the rack, he stirred the fire until it blazed, then returned the tool to its hook.

"Thinking about the case?" she asked, striving for a light tone.

"Not remotely." Hetheridge rose. "You look a bit better."

"I am." Under his gaze, Kate felt herself go shy. She was grateful for the study's dim lighting, in case she blushed beneath the strain of so much compassion. "Sorry I went to pieces on you.

Balancing the boys and my job is tough enough without a new responsibility. I didn't figure Dylan for father of the year, but I thought … Never mind. Now I have no choice but to go it alone."

"There is another choice."

"I've already thought of that. But no. I'm thirty-one. I might not get another shot at motherhood. Even if it's bollixed up, I'd better take it."

"I meant there was another choice besides going it alone." Hetheridge drew himself up. "Marry me."

"What?"

He cleared his throat. "I am asking you to do me the honor of becoming my wife."

Kate stared at him. Her controlled, ever-correct chief didn't flinch from her gaze. He looked as if he couldn't believe the words that had issued from his mouth—but would go to the block rather than do something as ungallant as take them back. Instead, he waited for her to speak, hardly seeming to breathe.

Kate never counted on pity from others, but that didn't stop her from dealing it out, especially when awash in gratitude. This eternal bachelor, relic of a vanished era, had been kind to her. Now he needed rescuing from his own good intentions.

"You're as bad as Bhar." She managed a believable laugh. "Lucky for you, I can take a joke. Us married? And all living here? With Henry breaking your antiques, and Ritchie camped in front of the telly, and a baby on the way? My mum would resurface when she heard the news. You'd have to open your wallet twice a month to keep her away." Kate gave Hetheridge a playful shove in the chest, like she would have done to Bhar, had he posed an equally preposterous suggestion. "Makes marrying Madge Comfrey worth a rethink, doesn't it?"

Hetheridge released his breath, giving Kate a weak smile. "I wouldn't go that far. Perhaps I spoke without a full under-standing of your family circumstances. But since I did make the offer, I would never …"

"Relax, Tony. I won't hold you to it. I'll be fine, I promise. And I'd better call a taxi."

"I'll drive you."

"That would be wonderful. Thanks for everything."

On impulse, Kate kissed Hetheridge, pressing her closed lips against his. She half expected his arms to go around her, but when she drew back, they were held stiffly at his sides. She couldn't interpret the expression in his eyes. Was it relief? Or disappointment?

CHAPTER SEVENTEEN

*H*etheridge returned to Wellegrave House around 2 a.m. to find Harvey waiting for him in the kitchen. The manservant, as he styled himself, was wrapped in an indigo silk robe embroidered with Chinese dragons. His hair was oily with some sort of overnight treatment, and his face glistened with moisturizer. He sat at the cook's table, nursing a mug of hot cocoa.

"Lord Hetheridge," Harvey leapt to his feet. "Is everything all right?"

"Fine. No need to worry."

"The young woman …?"

"My junior colleague, DS Wakefield. She suffered a death in the family, as it were, and required assistance. I brought her here until she calmed down, then took her home."

Harvey studied his face until Hetheridge felt a flare of anger. Blast the man, did he have to poke his nose into everything?

"Can I get you something?" Harvey asked.

"No." Hetheridge strode away without a backward glance.

When he reached his study, the fire had dwindled to red embers. Locking the door, Hetheridge went to the liquor cart, selecting a single-malt scotch. He filled a glass half full, reconsidered and filled it to the lip. Loosening his tie, he carried both glass and decanter to a chair, blew a sigh into the empty room, and began to drink.

* * *

HIS SKULL WAS ATTEMPTING to split open, roughly across the occipital bone, when he reached Scotland Yard at half-seven the next morning. Mrs. Snell had called him en route, as had Bhar. Thankfully, he'd insisted Kate take the day for bereavement leave, or he might be forced to reassure her, too. Irritated by the concern raised by his tardiness—good God, surely he'd been late before—Hetheridge stalked toward the lifts. Ignoring the nods and greetings, he gripped his briefcase and umbrella in each hand. A pair of all-black Hugo Boss sunglasses, borrowed from Harvey, shielded his eyes. Hetheridge, who was famously never ill, feared he might be sick if Mrs. Snell's breakfast dishes weren't cleared by the time he arrived.

The silver serving dishes were gone, he discovered upon entering his offices, but the odor of eggs, butter and coffee remained. Pausing in the doorway, Hetheridge swallowed hard. He could do this. Instruct Bhar to handle the Rowlands alone, take a stab at some paperwork or e-mails, and head home at noon.

Tucking his sunglasses into his overcoat, Hetheridge opened his office door. Bhar, checking his e-mail by phone, jumped up and tooted a noisemaker—the kind that sounded like breaking wind. He wore a sparkly party hat, and held out a pink one with sequins to Hetheridge.

"Happy sixtieth! I knew you were hiding at home, afraid of a surprise party! And I won't lie, I tried to organize one. There were no takers. Everyone's too afraid of you."

Pretending not to see the hat Bhar offered, Hetheridge put

down his briefcase and umbrella. A box wrapped in green- and burgundy-striped paper, topped with a gold ribbon, awaited him on his desk. It was exactly the size of a boxed brass clock—the sort engraved with name and years of service. Hetheridge stared at it. Could anyone think he needed another clock? Or was he so dull, so lifeless, no other token came to mind?

"Hey. Tony." Bhar studied his face. "You don't look good. Are you sick?"

"Hungover," Hetheridge sighed, removing his coat and dropping into the chair behind his desk.

Bhar raised his eyebrows. "Is it ... turning sixty?" His solicitude was authentic, and Hetheridge felt his foul mood lift.

"Only in the sense that a sixty-year-old man needs to drink less if he plans to work the next morning." Forcing a smile, he indicated the gift. "From you?"

"Forget it," Bhar said, scooping it up. "Just a stupid gag, that's all."

"I'd quite like a gag." Hetheridge took the package from Bhar's hands. "When you turn forty, it's all Grim Reapers and tequila. When you turn fifty, it's a quiet dinner. When you turn sixty, it's just whispers and health questions. If I see a Grim Reaper today, it'll quite likely be the genuine article. Unless there's one in here?" He shook the box, then pulled off the ribbon.

"No, don't open that, it's stupid," Bhar insisted, trying to pull the gift away. "I'll get you a real prezzie later. I don't want you to be angry."

"I'll only be angry if it's a clock, a pen set or a tie rack," Hetheridge said, tearing away the paper.

It was not a boxed brass clock. Nor was it an executive pen set, or a tie rack. It was, according to the breathless description on the package, a Real Molded Replica of an Asian porn star's nether regions—not just the usual orifice, but both, which the package copy seemed to regard as a major selling point. The photos depicted the porn star in question, wanton expression and flowing black hair, her legs arranged to put the real-life goods on display. This was helpful, since the pink silicone product visible through the box's transparent window hardly looked like a woman's parts. The card, taped to the box, said:

The only thing you don't have is a woman. – Paul

"Sorry," Bhar murmured, hands pressed against his cheeks like a repentant child. "I just wanted to make you laugh."

Hetheridge stared at the box. Then he did laugh, first a dry chuckle, then a real laugh, despite the vicious thudding in his head.

"Best birthday present I ever had. You keep it. You can recycle it when Superintendent Jackson's birthday comes around. He'll be overjoyed. And I won't be going home. After all the dodging and weaving the Rowlands have done, I'm rather eager to meet them. I don't suppose you have any of that stuff for the eyes? You know, that gets the red out?"

"I do indeed," Bhar grinned, patting his jacket pockets until he came up with the bottle. "Never pull an all-nighter without it. Sure you're up to this, Chief?"

"Quite sure. And hide that box before we leave. I don't want to come back to find Mrs. Snell dead on the carpet."

CHAPTER EIGHTEEN

Ginny Rowland was accustomed to control. She first demonstrated this by not being at home when Hetheridge and Bhar arrived, promptly at nine o'clock, on the doorstep of her Belgravia home. A maid answered, checked their credentials and led them into a mostly white, all contemporary living room. Hetheridge and Bhar waited for ten minutes before Ginny Rowland swept in—a tall brunette with long, well-shaped legs shown to best advantage by a short black skirt. A slim, balding man and two little white dogs also arrived, trailing in her wake.

"So sorry," she barked before either man could fully rise. "But then again, you've disrupted my week, haven't you? So it's only fair you wait on me."

With that, she disappeared again. The slim, balding man shot Hetheridge and Bhar an inscrutable glance before following her out of the living room. The dogs also paused, staring at the detectives with round black eyes. Then they each issued a defiant bark —an *en garde*, Hetheridge thought—before trotting after their mistress, nails clicking against the marble-tiled floor.

"Knockout legs," Bhar said to Hetheridge.

"I'd expect no less. Ever get confirmation Venture Perfect is a front for an escort service?"

"No. Thought I might lie about it."

"Better be sure. She's playing the high-handed lady to the hilt."

"That's what makes me sure." Bhar glanced around the living room, indicating a blood-red statue, twisted to resemble a pretzel, that served as a focal point in the otherwise antiseptic space. "Lots of modern art here. Splatter paintings. Bits of rubbish on pedestals. What do you make of it?"

"Don't understand it," Hetheridge said. "You mentioned checking on Charlie Fringate's solvency. Did you check on the Rowlands' finances, too?"

"I did. They're in debt up to their nose hairs. But would they stand to gain money by killing Malcolm Comfrey?"

"I don't know. Perhaps it was less a matter of enrichment and more a matter of not losing everything?" Hetheridge was surprised at how much he already favored the notion of Ginny Rowland as Comfrey's killer, on the strength of that three-second meeting. His instincts were fully engaged, and he was grateful. When he was intellectually curious, the ache of a hangover was far more bearable.

"That's unacceptable!" Ginny's voice drifted back to them, accompanied by the tap of high heels and doggie nails on smooth hard floors. "Your inefficiency has seriously jeopardized our banking relationship. I expect to be satisfied in this matter, and I anticipate an apology from your manager."

Ginny reentered the living room. Snapping her snow-white phone closed, she aimed a wide smile at Hetheridge and Bhar. "Now. Gentlemen. So wonderful to meet you at last."

Ginny Rowland was a stunning woman, fit for a photo shoot. She had creamy skin, shoulder-length hair so black it gleamed, and brilliant blue eyes. Her cheekbones were high, her nose petite, her lips plump and ideally shaped. In Hetheridge's estimation, she was a once-pretty woman who had been surgically optimized into a full-blown beauty. There was nothing of reality about her.

Ginny held out her hand to Hetheridge, red-lacquered nails bright against her pale skin. She seemed disappointed when he merely shook her hand; her posture seemed to anticipate he would bend and kiss it. Turning to Bhar, she put on the same bright, eager look all over again. The prostitute's gift, Hetheridge thought—to meet every new man, even in rapid succession, with that enthralled stare, as if she'd waited for him all her life.

Bhar, ever-quick on the uptake and shameless about using his foreign appearance for his own amusement, did kiss her hand, lingering over it with ridiculous ceremony.

"In my country," he announced in a thick Indian accent, "a blue-eyed woman is the rarest jewel."

If he conducts the entire interview with that accent, I'll throttle him, Hetheridge thought.

Ginny tossed a coquettish glance over her shoulder at the slim, balding man. He, along with the two little white dogs—probably Chihuahuas, but Hetheridge was no judge—had rejoined them.

"Listen to this, Burt. Flattery from Scotland Yard. Something for my memoirs, wouldn't you agree?"

Shrugging, Burt Rowland leaned against the snowy marble fireplace, arms folded across his chest. He seemed content to let his wife blaze forth unassisted.

"So where exactly is your native country?" Ginny asked, smiling on Bhar.

"Clerkenwell," Bhar admitted, reassuming his normal way of speaking. "But believe me, you'd be pretty rare there, too. I'm Detective Sergeant Paul Bhar."

"Bhar?" she repeated, smile disappearing. "The one who demanded we return from Provence? I thought I had you sacked."

"Not quite. But I did receive a severe reprimand," Bhar said cheerfully. "A lesson I won't soon forget."

"Are you the same detective who told poor Jules you were in the Taliban?"

"Received a written reprimand for that," Bhar said.

Ginny's red lips parted in a dangerous smile. She transferred her gaze to Hetheridge. "And you're the gentry, correct?"

"Anthony Hetheridge."

"That's right. Scotland Yard's own baronet. Or knight—that's it, isn't it? My goodness. You must have collared an awfully dangerous criminal for the Queen to bestow that title on you. Good for you! Do I call you Sir Anthony?"

"Just Anthony is fine." Smiling, Hetheridge held her gaze as if entranced by her beauty. "Terrible thing, letting titles get in the way. People are much more interesting without them. May we sit down?"

"Of course." Thawing visibly, Ginny shot another strange, triumphant glance at Burt. She seemed to enjoy receiving male attention in front of her husband, and determined to ensure he didn't miss a single nuance.

"Make yourselves comfortable." Ginny indicated the sofa. "No! Down! Down, Gerard! You, too, Lexie! Dirty paws! No dirty paws on my sofa! Burt, for God's sake," she barked again, switching back to that harsh, demanding tone, "help me with these dogs!"

With a sigh, Burt unfolded himself from his position against the fireplace. He plucked the dogs off the sofa amid a torrent of yapping protests. Then, with a fluffy white dog tucked beneath each arm, he exited the room.

"We'll need your husband back, I'm afraid," Hetheridge said, locking eyes with Ginny. Despite the police-procedural simplicity of his words, he allowed his tone and expression to send a different message: Not that I wouldn't rather concentrate every ounce of my attention on you.

"Let me help him crate the dogs," Ginny whispered, "and we'll be right back." With a conspiratorial wink, she click-clacked away after her husband.

"Brilliant," Bhar said, cuffing Hetheridge on the shoulder. "And she was doing her best to insult you. Wish I had that much self-control."

"I'll keep bringing you to visit Lady Margaret until you do," Hetheridge said. "When the Rowlands return, you'll conduct the interview. Let me break in when the moment is right."

* * *

GINNY AND BURT ROWLAND sailed through the initial phase of the questioning. Ginny soon loosened up, even toward Bhar. She enjoyed the experience of answering one man's questions while another—Hetheridge—maintained meaningful eye contact, and a third, Burt, absorbed it all. Midway through her discussion of the abortive engagement party—which matched the accounts given by Madge, Jules, Kevin Whitley and Charlie Fringate—the Rowlands' maid arrived to serve tall, mint-garnished glasses of lemonade. Observing the maid, whose nondescript face and dumpy figure said much about Ginny's tolerance for rivals, Hetheridge accepted the lemonade and took a sip. It was laced with vodka. Under ordinary circumstances, he would have swallowed one mouthful, then put the glass aside. Today, grateful for hair of the dog, he had every intention of drinking it down.

"We've heard a lot about how Malcolm Comfrey treated Kevin Whitley," Bhar was saying. "What did you make of the exchange?"

Ginny shrugged. "Malcolm hated weakness. Kevin is weak. He's an ideal target for a heat-seeking missile like Mal. Mal despised Jules, too, but not as much. Weakness in women he could tolerate, I suppose. Maybe he just considered it part of the natural order." Her eyes narrowed, but more with cold amusement than feminist outrage. "Of course, Mal fancied himself the strongest, most ruthless alpha male on the planet, and we poor little femmes were nothing next to him. Wonder if he still felt so big and bad when someone was beating his brains out?"

"What do you make of the way Comfrey was murdered?" Hetheridge interjected. Bhar, alert for the moment when Hetheridge would break in, swallowed his own query so well, the switch in interrogators seemed choreographed.

Ginny rewarded Hetheridge with a dazzling smile. "You want to trip me up!" she teased, shaking a finger at him. Her legs shifted, upper thigh rubbing against upper thigh beneath her short black skirt. It was a move too provocative for Hetheridge— or Bhar, or Burt Rowland—to miss, although none of the men overtly acknowledged it.

"But surely, Anthony," Ginny continued, "you realize Madge and Jules have told me everything. I heard all about poor Madge finding Mal in the study with a poker through his eye socket. At first I was shocked. Then it was all I could do to keep from laughing. Mal was a right git. If anyone deserved a fatal beating, it was him."

"That seems to be the consensus," Hetheridge said. "What stopped you from giving it to him?"

Ginny took a sip of her lemonade. Setting down her glass, she stretched, pushing those long, perfect legs out before her.

"I'm not really a hands-on sort of girl these days," she said at last. "Mal was a pill. An arse. A bloody bore whose only virtue was a genius for making money. That's why Burt and I tolerated him. The same way you tolerate a cash machine, even if it has trouble reading your card. As long as the money keeps coming out, fine. But if some punter gets angry and smashes it with a hammer, you don't mourn the loss. You just go looking for a brighter, shinier Cashpoint."

"Is that how you thought of Malcolm Comfrey during your affair with him? A Cashpoint machine?" Hetheridge waited a beat for the words to sink in, then added in Burt's direction, "Your pardon, Mr. Rowland. A murder investigation always churns up private details. And of course I refer to an affair that occurred before you met and married your wife."

Burt, still inscrutable, did not respond. But Ginny went colder, from her immobile forehead down to her plump red lips.

"Yes, that's precisely how I thought of Mal," she said. "A man with money to lavish on me while his wife reared their daughter, and managed their home, and maintained his reputation in the community. I didn't know Madge then—one of life's little ironies that I know her now. But I imagine if she and I had met during the affair, she would have asked me to wear out the cruel bugger before sending him home—and pick his pocket while I was about it."

"Fascinating conversation to imagine," Hetheridge said with a trace of genuine humor. In his opinion, Ginny believed what she was saying. She thought Madge would have reacted not as a woman scorned, but as a drudge grateful for respite. But it was hard to be sure what was true and what was artificial when interrogating a creature as self-obsessed as Ginny Rowland.

"Would it have mattered to her, do you think," Hetheridge asked. "If Madge had also known you weren't merely the other woman, but also a prostitute working for a high-end escort service?"

Ginny shot a glance at Burt. There was a moment when Hetheridge thought he had gambled wrong, and would regret it. Then she laughed.

"Well. Sherlock Holmes lives," Ginny said. "Congratulations for making some twit at Venture Perfect blab to you. They were always jealous of my talent for reinvention. And no, I don't think Madge would have blinked an eye at my choice of profession. At our level, all women are prostitutes. We just charge a good deal more than the average bird on the stroll. And that reminds me," Ginny gave that dangerous smile again, "isn't there a slag assigned to this case? Madge told me about a girl detective, all bad clothes and bad hair and just a whiff of the East End. I'm dying to meet her. Wanted to see what sort of burden the Met has taken on to satisfy the bleeding hearts. Besides you, of course, Detective Bhar."

Hetheridge felt a stab of true anger, like a steel bolt punched through his skull. He controlled his expression with effort, taking an extra second or two to be sure his composure was solid. Bhar, to Hetheridge's pride, maintained his affable expression.

"I had no idea all women at your level, as you put it, are prostitutes," Hetheridge said in his blandest tone. "That destroys one of our working hypotheses. That Malcolm Comfrey was no longer content to treat you as an inferior, simply making cutting remarks in your presence. According to the hypothesis, he crossed the line by threatening to actually expose your past. Not to your husband, of course," Hetheridge nodded toward Burt, "who knew of your former career, and perhaps even met you through Venture Perfect. But if Comfrey threatened you with exposure to all of London society, as the hypothesis went, that would have been a threat worth committing murder to prevent. Unless, of course, your female friends on the committees, and in the clubs, and at the parties, all acknowledge themselves to be prostitutes in the broader sense. In that case, you would have no social standing to lose, and thus no reason to silence Malcolm Comfrey."

Ginny Rowland stared at Hetheridge. Nothing about her face changed. But something in her eyes, some inner darkness, seemed to lash out at him. Beside her, Burt's expression finally shifted from unreadable to hostile, like a stupid dog catching on at last.

"You think you're so smart." Ginny's tone could have wilted roses. "So plummy and upper crust and male. Like you see everything, and understand everything, and no detail escapes your all-seeing eye. You know nothing," she spat. "I know more than Scotland Yard ever will about this case. I know who did it. I know why. And I see no reason to share what I know with a pair of incompetents like you."

"If you have any information, Mrs. Rowland, you're obligated to tell us," Bhar began, "under pain of ..."

"I take it back," Ginny cut across him in a falsely bright voice. "Don't know a thing. Now I've answered all your questions. So unless you have a search warrant, why don't you get the hell out of my house, Sir Anthony?"

"It's Lord Hetheridge, actually," he said, rising and giving her a small smile. "Ninth Baron of Wellegrave. But I wouldn't expect you to understand which title goes with a barony. Chief Superintendent Hetheridge is a perfectly adequate manner of address. Hopefully it will be easy for you to remember, when DS Bhar and I return."

CHAPTER NINETEEN

$\mathcal{K}$ate had no intention of taking more than one day of the bereavement leave owed her. But that day got off to a bad start when she stayed in bed till noon, awakening to a phone call from Henry's school, informing her he'd been skiving off again. That news started Kate on the tangent of trying to find Henry a local fencing instructor. After studying websites dedicated to the art of swordplay, then re-watching the *Star Wars* movies at deafening volume, Henry had decided fencing was the only sport for him. And having promised it, Kate had learned that karate, basketball and chess were the only options in their neighborhood.

I could ask Tony, she thought, and stopped.

She still couldn't believe he'd proposed marriage to her. Of course, when he said the words, she'd assumed he was operating from outrageous gallantry. After their is-that-a-sword-in-your-pocket encounter on the fencing mat, Kate knew he was physically attracted to her. So she'd concluded generosity of spirit, poured into lust, had boiled over into a marriage proposal he'd immediately regretted. And he had looked discomfited just before she chose to take it as a joke. Then he should have looked relieved, and he had—almost. His shoulders had dropped. His smile had been one-sided. It was several moments before he spoke again, on a subject bland enough for tea and cakes. The detective in Kate, accustomed to assessing suspects' mood and affect, would upon second review call it disappointment, not relief.

How bizarre that after her torrent of emotion for Dylan, Kate had spent the entire morning staring at the cracked ceiling above her bed, reviewing every word from Hetheridge, every look. During her relationship with Dylan, she'd frequently caught herself lecturing him in her mind. Did other people rehearse and rehash arguments while pushing a trolley round Tesco, or filling up on petrol, or tossing out junk mail? She'd won a thousand battles with Dylan that way.

Now, as she went about making his final arrangements, she found herself cataloguing her entire brief history with Hetheridge. Talking to herself in her own head about the "plonker affair," as Bhar called it; the night Hetheridge, handsome in evening dress, pulled up to her curb; the time he'd contradicted Lady Margaret's advice to cut her hair. As a child Kate had learned not to confide in her mother or sister, speaking the secrets of young womanhood only to herself. So she didn't find it strange when she admitted to herself, as she folded Henry's heap of white T-shirts and briefs, Hetheridge was quite attractive enough to take to bed. Various scenarios on that topic intruded on her thoughts with surprising frequency.

Girlishly agonizing over whether a man harbored singular feelings for her was unfamiliar to Kate. Her type—the Dylans of the world—were far too engaged in witticisms and world-weariness to cherish tender emotions for others. Yet while loading Tesco bags into her car's boot, she dissected even her most commonplace encounters with Hetheridge with surgical precision. If he cared for her, it mattered. It made his proposal all the more awkward, made their next meeting all the more charged.

And how do I feel about him? Kate asked herself, turning the key in the ignition. *He's my boss, we hail from alternate realities, in seven months I'll give birth to a dead man's baby.* All the reasons she and Hetheridge weren't together, and could never be together, stacked up in Kate's head like a brick wall. From behind its comforting mass, the answer came easily. *I fancy him like mad.*

* * *

KATE CALLED Mrs. Snell the next morning to say she would be taking another bereavement day. Dylan's arrangements, though simple, took a surprising amount of time and legwork—transferring his remains to a mortuary, arranging for a cremation and choosing an urn. By the time she arrived home, it was past six, and she'd received no messages from work. When her mobile finally rang, it was ten o'clock. Cassie and Henry were already in bed, and Kate and Ritchie were watching a pirate movie on DVD. Ritchie, his lips moving soundlessly in sync with the dialogue, ignored the ringing, but Kate hurried to answer her mobile, taking it into the kitchen where she had a modicum of privacy.

"Kate?" It was Bhar. He sounded excited.

"Hey, Paul. Something new on the case?"

"Yeah. I meant to call you yesterday, but I had a lot of paperwork to finish, and a thousand e-mails. Anyway—you want me to break down the last two days chronologically, or in order of significance?"

"Chronologically," Kate said.

"Okay. Yesterday, the old man and I interviewed Ginny and Burt Rowland. She admitted to being a former escort and having an affair with Malcolm Comfrey. Burt didn't say much of anything, but his wife's past came as no surprise to him. My Lord got Ginny's back up, and she announced she knew who killed Comfrey, and why. But she wouldn't be telling the stiffs at Scotland Yard how or why, no sir."

"Course not," Kate said.

"Next thing. This morning, Kevin Whitley came clean about why he went back inside the Comfrey house just before the murder. He left his gear in Jules's bedroom—weed and some heroin. He denies sharing it with Jules or selling it on the streets. He claims it was his, for his own personal use, and he's never dealt. Anyway, citing a dearth of material evidence and a lack of priors, Whitley's solicitor got him released on bond late this afternoon."

"Good for him."

"Yes. Now. Feel like suiting up and zipping over to Belgravia for the party?"

"What party?" The small hairs on the back of Kate's neck rose.

"The party at the Rowlands," Bhar said. "Someone emptied a gun full of hollow point bullets into Ginny Rowland's back. Her maid found her dead, face down on the living room rug. It's not white anymore. And little red doggie prints are everywhere."

Kate blew out her breath. "Wow. Maybe she really did know who killed Comfrey, and why."

"And maybe she tried turning that information to her financial advantage. Think Comfrey's killer is still trying to clean up his or her mess?" Bhar asked.

"Yeah," Kate said, already calculating how long it would take her to drive to Belgravia. "Be right there."

CHAPTER TWENTY

*W*hen Kate arrived in the Rowlands' neighborhood, panda cars encircled the house. The constabulary response was greater than the Comfrey murder had received— even the media vanguard had been driven out of filming range. Kate herself was obliged to park two streets down the block, then hoof it up to the Rowlands' house. She was also compelled to show her warrant card time and again, first to one constable and then to another, as if she were a parasite, intent on feeding off a real-life crime scene. It was a very different experience from riding in Hetheridge's Lexus—halted for no more than a few seconds before the uniforms scrambled to lift away barriers and wave them through. Hetheridge was known on sight; she was forced to prove her identity again and again.

I shouldn't complain, Kate thought, forcing a smile for the fifth constable who brusquely demanded to see her ID. *They're just preserving the scene for CID, the way they're charged to do.*

Cleared at last, Kate veered toward the house's side entrance. It was bright with halogen security lights, as well as ever-shifting blue strobes, and guarded by several uniformed officers. There she saw a familiar figure near the rubbish bins, speaking to a tall constable in a flapping black mack.

"Oi! Chief!" she called. "I made it!"

Hetheridge's head jerked toward her. Attired more casually than she'd ever seen him—black slacks, black polo shirt, and a wool jacket with a miniscule plaid pattern—he looked younger and better rested than when she'd seen him last. He didn't smile or lift a hand. Instead, he turned back to the tall constable, resuming the conversation.

Kate felt a twinge of worry. This would be awkward, after all. Perhaps she should venture into the house alone? Bhar was probably there, and she could glom onto him for support. Besides, the crime scene awaited, and it would be natural for her—the junior sergeant with everything to prove—to fling herself at the evidence in desperation to make a contribution.

Kate weighed her options. She strode up to Hetheridge and waited at his elbow like a latecomer at a cocktail party, determined to insinuate herself with the best people.

"Excellent custodianship of the scene. Good observations, too. Thank you very much," Hetheridge concluded, shaking the constable's hand. The tall young man looked both pleased and embarrassed. Finally, he shot a smile at Kate—a "You're my witness!" look—before flapping off toward his fellow officers. As the constable passed out of earshot, Hetheridge turned to Kate, eyes hooded, still unsmiling.

"Sergeant. I appreciate your presence. Are you certain you're ready to return to duty?"

"Wouldn't be anywhere else. This isn't a hot scene, is it?" she asked, guessing why the media had been driven so far back, and why the uniformed response had been so impressive.

"We don't know," Hetheridge said. "Burt Rowland burst in just as the first responders assessed the scene. He attacked an officer and had to be physically restrained by two others. He seems genuinely distraught over the death of his wife ..."

"But that doesn't mean he's not the shooter," Kate said. "Is he still here?"

"Under arrest, technically," Hetheridge said. "His hands have been swabbed for gun powder residue, and his shoes and clothing will be taken for analysis as soon as we finish his interrogation. Then we can decide whether to charge him with murder or release him."

"Blood on his clothing?" Kate asked.

"Lots. Not a splatter pattern, though, to the naked eye. Just a mass of blood absorbed into his coat and shirt when he lifted Ginny's body and tried to resuscitate her. Some of his own blood, too, from cuts and scrapes when he scuffled with the officers."

"Has anyone found the weapon?"

"Not yet. But come the dawn, we'll have constables walk the property from one end to the other and see if it turns up."

"Witnesses?"

Hetheridge shrugged. "At this point, I'll refrain from dignifying them with that term. Let's just say there are dozens of interested parties in the neighborhood queuing up to speak to the police. From what I can tell, they're mostly supplying complaints about what an unpleasant and inconsiderate neighbor Mrs. Rowland was."

"Can I see the body before we speak to Burt Rowland?"

"Absolutely." Opening the side door, Hetheridge held it for Kate until she entered ahead of him. Stepping into the Rowlands' mudroom, half of Kate's mind inventoried the details of her rapid-fire exchange with Hetheridge while the other half wondered what he was feeling. He had looked and sounded the same, and yet … something was different. Something was missing.

Hetheridge guided Kate through the mudroom and kitchen, then down a minimalist corridor, decorated with black and white photos in square black frames. Next came the living room, where Ginny Rowland was sprawled on the floor, about three meters from the foyer. Blood was everywhere—soaking her black dress, her hair, and the shag area rug that had once been white. Blood also pooled on the hardwood floor, congealing in spots, smeared and tracked in others. Large shoe prints were visible, like a sloppy red dance-step diagram, as were the doggie prints Bhar had mentioned. A long stream of animal tracks traveled across the cushions of the white sofa, each paw print as red and distinct as a lipstick print.

"Bhar said she was shot in the back," Kate said, frowning at the position of Ginny's body. Ginny's eyes were open, and she lay awkwardly on her side, one arm crumpled beneath her. Her chest was strangely asymmetric—a flat breast on the right, a round breast on the left. After a second, Kate realized that one of the bullets had pierced an implant, which had drained of saline or silicone as Ginny's body emptied of blood.

"Burt Rowland lifted her up, flipped her over and tried to perform mouth-to-mouth, according to the first responders," Hetheridge sighed. "No photos had been taken, of course. And as you can see from that smear of blood," he pointed, "Mr. Rowland obviously dragged her at least a meter from her original position. But hopefully the blood spatter team can use that," he pointed again at a faint red stippling on the sofa, "to determine exactly where she was standing when she was shot."

Kate nodded, ashamed to admit she was slightly nauseated by the powerful coppery odor. "Think it's the same killer who did Malcolm Comfrey?"

Hetheridge smiled for the first time, but it was a professional smile, never touching his eyes. "You tell me, Sergeant."

"Right." Kate folded her arms across her chest and studied the body. It was cold in the Rowlands' home, with a steady stream of icy air emitting from some hidden vent. She found herself rocking in an involuntary attempt to warm herself. "The Comfrey murder appears to be a crime of passion, at least to some extent. The degree of rage directed at him was made manifest by the killer's need to not only end his life, but to obliterate him—in that case, by rendering his face unrecognizable. This murder is more like an execution. The killer premeditated the act, came to Ginny Rowland's home to carry it out, and fired multiple times to make certain she died."

Hetheridge nodded. "So would you venture to call it a definite execution?"

"No." Kate continued to rock, hands and face growing colder. "A professional would have shot her in the head. This killer shot Ginny in the back. Several times, yes, but in the back. To me, that means the killer knew Ginny. And even though the perpetrator wanted Ginny dead, he or she wasn't an experienced-enough killer to look her in the eye and shoot her."

"My conclusions precisely. Thank you, Sergeant. We should proceed to questioning Burt Rowland now ..."

"Tony," Kate interrupted, holding his gaze. Of course, they weren't alone. There were constables just outside the living room, and sounds from the investigation intruded from every side—harsh male voices, footsteps, creaking floorboards, yappy dogs barking somewhere. But Kate was too at home in CID chaos to feel constrained by it, not even the stink of a fresh corpse. She couldn't allow this disconnection to persist between her and Hetheridge, not for another moment.

"Sergeant, it's imperative we continue without delay. I ..."

"Tony, this won't take a minute. I just want to say ..."

"Chief Hetheridge?" a uniformed officer asked from the corridor where they'd entered. His tone was apologetic, with an undercurrent of urgency. "I'm sorry to interrupt, but we have a situation outside."

"What situation?" Hetheridge demanded in that tone of command that came so naturally to him.

"Madge Comfrey and Jules Comfrey tried to gain access to the scene. They claim to be personal friends of the Rowlands and attempted to enter through a neighbor's back garden. Shall we arrest and hold them, sir?"

"No. This is a bit of a diplomatic situation, I'm afraid. Cut the wrong wire on this particular bomb and Scotland Yard will have another mountain of bad press to overcome. I'll deal with it. DS Wakefield, I believe DS Bhar is already with Mr. Rowland. Please join him and begin the questioning. I'll return as soon as I'm able."

* * *

BURT ROWLAND WAS BEING DETAINED, at least in the formal sense, in the dining room. The officers he had assaulted kept him under a watchful eye, two standing, another sitting on one of the high-backed chairs. All three officers appeared unharmed, except for blood smears on their uniforms, and the suggestion of a bruise forming on one man's cheek. Rowland, by contrast, sat deflated at the head of the table, shoulders sagging, legs apart, feet pointed in toward one another. His coat and tie had already been taken for the lab—both items, stiff with drying blood, were sealed in large plastic evidence bags. They rested bizarrely on the side-board, next to the china cups and saucers. Rowland's shirt, once pastel blue with a narrow stripe, was decorated with dark blots, like a Rorschach print awaiting interpretation.

Bhar stood at the periphery of the room, texting something into his smart phone. He looked cheered to catch sight of Kate, and gave her a wave. Finishing the message, he snapped his phone closed, stowing it in his pocket. Coming up close, he muttered in Kate's ear. "Did Our Lord give us permission to start?"

"Yep. Care to do the honors?"

"Burt's a wee bit hostile toward me just now. Maybe you should try your feminine wiles?"

Nodding, Kate took a deep breath, then started toward Burt.

He didn't look up as she approached, so she pulled out a dining chair, allowing it to drag across the floor. Bhar did the same, also with exaggerated slowness and noise, but Rowland still did not acknowledge their presence. His upper lip was cut and swollen. There was a plug of dried blood in one nostril, and his left eye looked pink and puffy.

"Mr. Rowland, I'm DS Kate Wakefield. This is DS Paul Bhar, whom I believe you've already met. I'm terribly sorry about everything you've suffered tonight, including your injuries."

"Sod off. Both of you," Burt said. His deep, resonant voice seemed incongruous coming from his slim, compact frame.

"I'm afraid we can't just leave you to grieve," Kate said. "We need to find out what happened to your wife. We ..."

"Sod off!" Burt screamed. Flecks of spittle hit Kate in the face, and she saw directly into Rowland's eyes—bloodshot whites, dilated pupils and a shine of terror. "You, your pet Paki, these gorillas, the whole lot! I won't speak to you without my solicitor! I won't say a goddamn thing!"

Bhar put a hand on Kate's shoulder. It was easy to interpret his nonverbal suggestion: de-escalate the situation. Leave for a while, then return, preferably with someone new in tow, like Hetheridge, who Burt might actually consent to talk to.

Wiping her face, Kate studied Burt. The uniformed officers had moved closer, exuding obvious and somewhat overstated menace on Kate's behalf, but she waved them back. Her instincts told her Burt wouldn't physically attack her, so she decided to try one more tack.

"Mr. Rowland," Kate said. "I can't imagine how you feel right now. I can only guess you wish you could go back in time and protect your wife. And even now, your most powerful impulse must be to protect her, and show loyalty toward her."

Burt stared at her, still rigid with fury. Slowly, his shoulders relaxed and he nodded, pressing a hand to his mouth.

"Yes," he said softly, voice ragged. He squeezed his eyes shut, rubbed at them and met Kate's gaze with a visible effort. "Yes," he repeated, stronger.

"But the desire to be loyal, and to keep her secrets, might be the very worst way to help your wife," Kate said. "Something she shared with you, especially in the last few days, might help us catch the person who did this to her. Please tell us everything. I promise, we have no interest in anything you disclose, except as it pertains to bringing her killer to justice."

She'd found the right words. Something in Burt's bearing changed, and though he remained silent for several more seconds, she knew he meant to cooperate, as soon as he mastered his emotions enough to speak.

"Ginny and I have endured some financial setbacks over the past two or three years," he began at last. "I think she was trying to solve things. She didn't want me involved. She told me ..." He stopped. "For this to make sense, I need to go back. Can I start at the beginning?"

"Please," Kate said.

"When our problems began," Rowland said, "I wanted to keep the matter private and solve it by any means necessary—sell our house, downsize our cars and vacations and so on. Ginny wouldn't have it. She thought if we gave up the trappings of wealth, and the aura of success—excess, really—we'd never recover our credibility." Rowland's eyes cut to Bhar. "You came in this house and called her a prostitute to her face, and she never blinked. She had tremendous strength. She wasn't ashamed of anything she'd done to get ahead. The only thing that ever scared her was the notion of sliding backward, back to the life she worked so hard to escape."

"I can understand that," Kate said, mostly to redirect Burt's attention before his hostility toward Bhar derailed the questioning again. "So did Ginny come up with a way to improve your finances?"

"Her first idea was to ask Malcolm for money. This was a few years ago, as I said, before he became so tightfisted, and we were all great friends. I was against it, nonetheless, but I let her have her head. God knows, I always did. And Malcolm laughed at her. Right in front of me, like he knew I wouldn't have the nerve to defend her. Malcolm laughed at Ginny and said he never loaned money to his friends, and if anything, she should be paying him to keep her past as an escort under wraps. I wanted to leave then, to walk away and pretend the request never happened, but when Ginny gets angry ..." Burt paused. "When Ginny got angry," he corrected himself, voice shaking, "there was no stopping her. She told Malcolm she knew a secret about him, one he'd pay dearly to hush up, and it would cost him half a million pounds to seal her lips on the subject."

"What secret?" Bhar asked, pen poised above his notepad.

Burt cut his eyes back to Bhar as if he'd forgotten his presence. "Jesus. Jesus, this can't be real. I must be dreaming," he whispered, pressing his hands to his face. "Can I have a drink? A whisky?"

"Not yet, I'm afraid," Kate said. "We can't allow you to consume alcohol while giving your statement. Besides, it might make you forget something. But as soon as we're done speaking, you can certainly have a drink. Or we can call a doctor to prescribe you a sedative."

Burt nodded numbly, gaze drifting toward the arched passage that led from the dining room to the living room, where Ginny Rowland lay.

"Mr. Rowland," Kate prompted, "did Malcolm Comfrey pay half a million pounds to silence your wife?"

Burt looked surprised. "What? No—no, of course not. He called her bluff. At first he was angry, and demanded to know what she'd dug up. Then, when she told him, he laughed. Said he wouldn't be the one to pay the price, and if Ginny wanted to torpedo two or three other lives, she was welcome to do so."

"What was the secret?" Kate asked.

"One of those things I never would have noticed. But Ginny notices—noticed everything. She could have been a professor at university, if life had been different. She never missed a detail. Ginny and Madge were on some committee or other that was trying to raise awareness about blood donation. Influential donors were supposed to demonstrate how easy and painless giving blood can be. Ginny forced me to agree to giving blood— I'd never done it—and Madge managed to herd in Malcolm and Jules, too.

"I was sick and miserable throughout. Malcolm, Madge and Jules did better. They were sitting in their lounge chairs, watching their blood slide down tubes and fill up plastic bags, while a nurse made the rounds. She was marking the bags with blood-type stickers. She marked Malcolm and Madge's, and had just put a sticker on Jules's bag when Jules asked Malcolm a question. She called him 'Daddy,' and the nurse stopped what she was doing. She looked at the sticker, then went and rechecked Malcolm's bag, and Madge's. I didn't notice, but Ginny caught it like one of those cadaver-sniffing dogs." Burt gave a strained chuckle at his grotesque choice of words. "Ginny actually examined the sticker on each blood bag. It was all she talked about on the way home, how the nurse had looked from Jules to Malcolm, like she wanted to ask a question but thought better of it. Then Ginny got on the Internet and researched blood types and heredity. She woke me up out of a sound sleep to tell me Jules Comfrey couldn't be Malcolm Comfrey's daughter. Their blood types made it impossible."

"How could she be sure of that? Mrs. Rowland wasn't a doctor," Bhar said.

"She said it was simple," Burt replied. "Malcolm was type A, and Madge was type O, but Jules was B negative. It's impossible for them to produce a B negative child. Therefore, either Jules was adopted—and she wasn't—or she was fathered by someone other than Malcolm."

As Bhar's pen flew over the page, Kate considered this. Something was nagging at the back of her mind. Some bit of information that had seemed inconsequential or silly when she received it—like a mild joke, or a weird dream.

"And when Ginny gave this information to Malcolm Comfrey, he laughed and refused to pay her?" Kate asked.

Burt nodded.

"Do you think he already knew?"

"I don't know. Malcolm always maintained control. Even when he went for the jugular, he kept his voice steady. Kept a bastard smile on his face. All I know is, he told Ginny if she dropped her bombshell, as he put it, it would be Madge and Jules —and maybe the mystery father—who suffered from the revelation. He'd been disappointed in Jules almost since she was born, or so he told us, and the discovery she wasn't actually his came as a great relief."

"Burt!" a female voice cried. Jules Comfrey entered, face blotchy and eyes red. "God, Burt, I'm so sorry! I don't understand why this is happening to us!"

Hetheridge appeared on her heels, with Madge Comfrey just behind him. "I will allow the Comfreys to speak briefly with Mr. Rowland," he said, addressing Kate, Bhar and the uniformed officers. "This breach of procedure occurs under my authority. However, I will not allow them to venture any deeper into the crime scene than—Ms. Comfrey!" he snapped, as Jules darted toward Burt Rowland with the clear intention of embracing him. "His clothing is evidence! Do not touch him!"

Jules Comfrey stopped, drawing up just short of Burt. Kate, only a short distance away, studied the young woman more carefully than ever before. Jules was of middling height, slender, with fine-boned features that had always struck Kate as aristocratic. She had her mother's thick, dark hair. But her best feature was her long-lashed, finely shaped, ice blue eyes.

CHAPTER TWENTY-ONE

"**W**hat do you mean, evidence?" Jules cried, rounding on Hetheridge. "Ginny's been murdered and you're treating Burt like a suspect? Burt? How bloody stupid are you? Is this all you know how to do, turn up at crime scenes and accuse the family? Why aren't you out on the street finding the person who did this? It's probably the same person who killed my father!"

"That is quite enough," Hetheridge boomed. Jules's mouth, open for another volley, snapped shut. No one else spoke or moved. Silence wrapped around the room like a shroud.

Hetheridge's gaze shifted from Madge to Jules, then back again. What felt like several seconds ticked by before he spoke.

"Ms. Comfrey, you and your mother have already been indulged far beyond the norm. This ends now. I allowed you to enter the crime scene because I have been charged with the thankless, and apparently impossible, task of pacifying your infantile temperaments without making it obvious you are both suspects. But hear me now: you are each under intense scrutiny. And this display—attempting to slip into the scene before the victim has even been removed—does nothing to enhance your

179

appearance of innocence. Put another toe out of line and I'll arrest you both under suspicion of murder, obstruction of justice, and interference with a crime scene."

"You wouldn't ..." Madge began.

"I will and I shall, if you test me," Hetheridge cut across her. "You've already gone above my head at the Yard and it got you nowhere. Your influence is limited, and now at its end. I have no fear of you, Madge."

Madge stared at Hetheridge with an expression Kate could only interpret as rage. It seemed genuine, pure as platinum. Then it was gone, replaced by pain, hurt and the warmth that knows it will be rejected.

"No fear," Madge said. "Nor any love, either, it seems."

"Mrs. Comfrey," Hetheridge said. He allowed her name to hang between them. "I am here in my professional capacity to seek justice on behalf of Malcolm Comfrey. And now Ginny Rowland. No other reason." He turned back to Jules Comfrey. "You demanded to see Burt Rowland. You've seen him. And now, rather than contaminate this scene further, I'd like you and your mother to accompany me to New Scotland Yard. There we can revisit your testimonies and be certain no detail has been overlooked."

* * *

AFTER HETHERIDGE DEPARTED with the Comfreys in tow, Burt Rowland asked for a break. It was his third since his discovery of Ginny's body, but no one complained. A uniformed officer matter-of-factly escorted Burt to the lavatory. Violent death, as Kate herself had recently learned, led to a full-body purge—not just for the corpse, but for those left behind, too. It was not uncommon for even an admitted murderer to have his or her confession interrupted by a weak bladder, loose bowels or a violent case of the dry heaves.

"I've never seen Hetheridge so angry," Kate said to Bhar, too low for the other officers to hear.

"That wasn't anger. That was a performance," Bhar returned from the side of his mouth.

"What do you mean?"

"Think about it. Hetheridge wasn't chosen as the Yard's liaison to the wealthy and powerful because he licks them up the legs. He was chosen because he strokes them with one hand and smacks them with the other. There are dozens of detectives willing to French kiss privileged arse from here to the Isle of Wight, without a pause for floss or Chap Stick. But the old man's the only one who's willing to put the strap to their bums when the occasion demands it."

"Makes sense," Kate said, again impressed by Bhar's insight. "I thought he was about to lose it."

"Something none of us will ever see, I suspect."

"Why?"

Bhar turned his grin on Kate. "Because of the blue blood in his veins. His sort doesn't reveal their emotions. I've always figured if you trace the chief's paternity back to the first Baron of Wellegrave, you'll find a right bastard fully in touch with his need to bonk and his need to kill. But every baron thereafter was a little paler, a little politer, and a little more concerned with which fork to use. Maybe Our Lord is a throwback to that first ruthless git. But he's constrained by the emotional equivalent of Chinese foot binding. Put him in a situation that requires courage without sentiment, and he's your man. Put him in a situation that requires him to express an actual feeling, and he'll probably end up saying nothing at all."

"I'm sorry." Burt reappeared in the dining room, his uniformed officer-escort trailing behind. Burt's face was white, his eyes red-rimmed. He had clearly used his lavatory trip to break down for what Kate suspected would be the first of many times, and his deep voice trembled when he spoke again.

"I'm all right now. Ready to tell you anything. Anything to help Ginny."

"You mentioned how your wife tried to blackmail Malcolm Comfrey with the news his presumed daughter wasn't actually his," Kate said. "You went on to say he called her bluff, as you put it, and refused to pay to suppress the information. Can I assume Ginny let the matter drop when she realized there was no profit in revealing her deduction?"

"Of course." Burt dropped back into the high-backed chair he'd occupied before, knees touching and hands clasped in his lap, like a forlorn child. "Ginny loved Jules. She thought she was a mixed-up kid, and downright foolish when it came to men, but Ginny loved her all the same. Her relationship to Madge was a bit more … grown up. They were friends, but there was some female rivalry there, too. Ginny might have told Madge she knew the truth about Jules. I don't know. Ginny only confided one thought in ten to me."

"Why was that?" Kate asked, taking a seat at the dining table.

"Knowledge is power. And Ginny rarely gave away power. That made her more alluring than any woman I'd ever known."

"You said Mrs. Rowland's attempt to blackmail Malcolm Comfrey happened some time ago. Was she planning to black-mail Comfrey's killer this time?" Bhar asked. "She told me and the chief she knew exactly who killed Comfrey, and why."

"I think that's what happened," Burt said, voice cracking. "I wanted to stay home with her tonight, but she told me to get out. She said, 'For God's sake, Burt, go to the cinema or your club or have a wank, but get out.' She said, 'This is my business and you'll thank me when I'm done.' I didn't argue. I just left. Went to my gym and worked out, then had dinner. Half a bottle of wine, too. Wasted enough time to give her all the space she needed. I knew if I came home and found her in a triumphant mood, she'd reward me for my obedience."

Kate suppressed a grimace. Now that Burt's defenses had

crumbled, she had a feeling he might reveal greater intimacies. Did she really want to hear what a submissive type like Burt considered a reward from his ruthless, professionally seasoned bride?

Kate pressed on. "Who do you think Ginny attempted to blackmail this time?"

"Had to be Ivy," Burt sighed.

Kate and Bhar exchanged a glance. He was getting all this down in his notes, writing as fast as an old-fashioned shorthand secretary.

"Ivy who?" Kate asked, her chair scraping across the floor as she pulled it closer to Burt.

"Ivy Helgin," Burt said, still in that sad, disconnected tone. "Malcolm's mistress. The woman who wanted Malcolm to leave Madge and marry her. I didn't see it at first. I thought Ivy was a good-time girl who knew her place, but Ginny set me straight. Said Ivy had smarts and ambition. Said Ivy was a girl on the rise. Said she wouldn't waste her time on a man like Mal—paunchy, wrinkly and in need of a boatload of Viagra to get it up—unless marriage was on the table."

Kate took a moment to process this. Bhar's pen scraped over his notebook paper. He turned the page, resumed his hasty writing, and Kate spoke again.

"Tell me about Ivy."

"Ivy," Burt exhaled. His demeanor had become one of a hypnotized subject—soft-spoken, unguarded, willing to spell out the answer to any and all questions. "She's about twenty-five. Tall. Red hair. Legs that go all the way up. Nice laugh, nice smile. Ginny said Ivy sold herself as Little Red Riding Hood. You know —tease the wolf with a covered basket and lots of 'my, what a big one you have.' And Mal had to buy what was in her basket, because he'd already conquered everything else in his path. He had the perfect homemaker and society wife in Madge. So perfect, he could have stood for Parliament. He'd made money.

He'd wedged his foot into the outer circle of high society. But he'd also grown older, and weaker, and needed a saucy young rump to bring him alive."

"Yet he wouldn't divorce Madge and marry Ivy?"

Burt gave a short laugh. "Don't you know the law? They say reform's on the way, but the fact is, in this country, at this minute, an injured wife stands to collect far beyond her due. A straying husband puts both hands on the block and prays the law only chops off one. Malcolm couldn't have endured that. Losing so much to Madge, permanently, just to make his mistress an honest woman."

"And you think that turned Ivy homicidal?" Kate asked.

"Isn't that what turns everyone homicidal? Sex or money?" Burt shrugged.

"But Ivy wasn't included on the guest list the night of the engagement party," Bhar pointed out. "The party for Jules and Kevin that went so wrong, just a few hours before Comfrey was murdered."

"You think Ivy had never been in Mal's house?" Burt asked. "Think he wouldn't welcome her if she just wanted to come over for a chat?"

"With Madge upstairs?" Kate reminded him, unconvinced.

"Well, Ivy was Mal's administrative assistant," Burt said off-handedly, as if he had already mentioned it. "She turned up from time to time with legitimate business concerns. How could Madge have known the difference?"

"Detectives!" a male voice called from behind Kate and Bhar.

Lip curling in frustration, Kate turned to see the tall constable Hetheridge had complimented—the one with the flapping black coat. Inside the Rowland house, he looked pastier and blonder, with wide eyes, wet hair and a continuous drip off his mack, as if he'd spent hours stationed in the rain.

"Can't this wait?" Kate snapped, impatience unconcealed.

Didn't the constable realize the interview with Burt Rowland had reached a critical juncture?

"I don't think so," the constable said. "Chief Hetheridge told us to search for evidence. I walked every meter of this property twice. On my second walk, I found this." He held up a green plastic watering can.

Before Kate indulged her temptation to verbally abuse the dripping constable, Bhar leapt to his feet. Peeking inside the watering can, he stiffened. Then, withdrawing a blue latex-free glove from his jacket pocket, he pulled it on his hand and reached inside the can. When his gloved hand reappeared, his thumb and forefinger were attached, pincer-style, to a black 9 mm pistol.

"Oh, no," Burt breathed. His eyes went wide. "Is that what killed Ginny?"

"Quite likely," Bhar said, his gaze meeting Kate's. "And if it has prints, we might have our first big break in the case."

CHAPTER TWENTY-TWO

*H*etheridge drove his Lexus back to New Scotland Yard, allowing Madge and Jules Comfrey to follow behind in a panda car with the lights off. He had offered the police conveyance with no expectation they would accept it—he'd anticipated outrage at the mere suggestion, and a demand to drive themselves. Instead, the pair agreed with a surprising lack of indignation. And it was that meek acceptance of a ride that made him examine both women again, using the pretense of an apology—how very sorry he was about losing his temper—to touch each woman's hand and stare into her eyes.

Madge's skin was clammy. She seemed on the verge of exhaustion, breathing slowly and clutching Hetheridge as if she appreciated the support. Jules, by contrast, was breathing rapidly and in constant motion. She babbled something over his apology, some recycled list of Scotland Yard's flaws in general, and Hetheridge's flaws in particular, but he ignored the words. Of more interest to him was Jules's trembling hands and dilated pupils.

Drug tests, he thought on the drive back to Scotland Yard. His iPod, connected to the car stereo, blared a Bach piano concerto his brain knew so intimately, he could hear it, yet not hear it, as his mind sifted the facts of the case. Yes, he would need to administer drug tests to both Madge and Jules Comfrey the moment they arrived. Of course, it would be his hide peeled off and knitted into a running suit, rather tight in the shoulders and short in the leg, for Superintendent Deaver to wear round the gym, if those drug tests proved negative. But they wouldn't. Experience assured him Jules's, at least, would come back positive for some stimulant. And that might go a long way toward explaining how she'd summoned the nerve to storm a crime scene.

But why didn't Madge stop her? Had she no control over her daughter whatsoever?

He didn't relish the notion of interviewing Madge at length. He'd given her little or no thought in the last twenty years—just another failed relationship from that period in his late thirties to early fifties, when he'd toyed with the notion of selecting an appropriate woman to start a family with. But it was always wrong, always forced, and he knew why: because he was always wrong, always forced, too intent on his career, too protective of all the male clichés: space, freedom, privacy. He hadn't wanted to share himself, hadn't understood how any man—or woman, for that matter—could be interested in signing on for such merciless emotional exposure. Once the miseries of childhood were escaped, once a path in the professional jungle was hacked clear, why subject oneself to an endless round of scrutiny and disappointment?

He'd proposed to Madge for a number of reasons. Because she was attractive, because she was appropriate, and because they'd shared a physical connection so intense, it mitigated dozens of lesser complaints. But mostly he'd proposed because his mother had spent the previous family Christmas lunch excoriating him. According to Lady Hetheridge, even Lord Ligon's famously queer son had done his duty to his forbears, married, and produced three children. Why couldn't her embarrassment of a son do the same?

A month later, his mother had died. Two months later, Hetheridge had proposed to Madge, delighting her with an eye-popping Cartier solitaire. He wondered if she still had it; after breaking the engagement, he hadn't asked for it back. He hoped —without much hope—that she didn't believe he had used her coldly, and dropped her cruelly, after the initial attraction waned. The words had come easily when he proposed to her, because they sprang from an intellectual desire to do his duty. He hadn't humiliated himself with a few awkward utterances, the way he had with Kate.

What did I say? Something about doing me an honor, Hetheridge thought. *Good God, no wonder she laughed. Didn't even tell her I loved her.*

Of course, he'd never said it to Madge, either. But with Kate, even if he'd been unable to force out the words, he knew it was true. Not through experiential wisdom, or any evidence he could bring to bear. He knew it the way he knew he was right-handed.

Something was off—discordant—about the Bach concerto. After a moment, Hetheridge's brain returned fully to the present: the road before him, the shine of headlights in the distance, and the trill of his mobile on the seat beside him. Muting the music, he put the phone to his ear.

"Hetheridge."

"Chief, it's me. Kate. Have you made it to the Yard?"

"I'll be there in two or three minutes. Why?"

"Bhar and I have new information for you. Can you put off questioning the Comfreys?"

"Not possible."

"I don't mean for the whole night, just until I can get there. I'd like to bring you up to speed in person."

"Tell me now."

Kate sighed. "First of all, one of the constables found a 9

millimeter pistol in a watering can in the front garden. We dispatched a courier to take it directly to Forensic Services."

"Excellent. Who found it?"

"The tall one. MacAllister, I think his name is."

"Indeed. Sharp young man. I'll write him a letter of commendation. What else?"

"Burt Rowland has a theory about who killed his wife and Malcolm Comfrey. He thinks it was Comfrey's mistress, Ivy Helgin. She was also Comfrey's administrative assistant. I'd like to track her down first thing tomorrow and see what she has to say."

"I agree. What's the presumptive motive?"

"According to Rowland, Ms. Helgin would have killed Comfrey because he refused to divorce Madge and marry her. Then she would have killed Ginny Rowland because she was trying to blackmail her over the Comfrey murder. Apparently, the Rowlands had significant cash flow problems, and Ginny tried her hand at blackmail once before."

"Good work. Ivy Helgin—is that H-e-l-g-i-n? Fine. I'll drop the name in front of Madge and Jules and see if it raises any reaction. Ah—the Yard's in sight."

"Chief." Kate sounded odd. "There's one more thing."

Hetheridge steeled himself. For reasons he couldn't articulate intellectually, he wanted to sidestep this conversation. He didn't anticipate unkindness from Kate. He didn't even expect a recitation of why she didn't share his feelings and never could, beginning with her youth and beauty and ending with his decrepitude and lack of personal charm. But however she chose to truncate this awkwardness between them, he was not above using his position as her superior officer to forestall it.

"DS Wakefield, unless what you have to say pertains directly to the case, I'm afraid it will have to wait."

"It does pertain to the case." Kate still sounded odd. "The first person Ginny Rowland tried to blackmail was actually Malcolm

Comfrey. She'd found out Malcolm wasn't Jules's father, and she tried to use that information to extort a half-million pounds. But Comfrey called her bluff. He said the revelation would hurt Jules and Madge more than him, so it amounted to nothing."

Hetheridge pulled up to the Yard's gatehouse, lowered his car window, and nodded at the guard on duty. Without requesting identification, the guard hit a button, and the reflective white barrier gate began to lift.

"So Jules isn't Malcolm Comfrey's daughter. And you consider that significant to the case? Perhaps as a motive?" Hetheridge asked, parking in New Scotland Yard's starkly illuminated, mostly empty lot. Fog swirled along the ground, thinner and patchier than usual. The night air, creeping in through Hetheridge's open window, was cold and damp.

"Not sure exactly how it fits in. Still thinking about that angle," Kate said. "Ginny discovered the truth about Jules's paternity during a blood drive. Apparently, Malcolm and Madge Comfrey's blood types are A and O. Jules's is B negative. The combination of type A and type O can't produce a B negative. Since there's no doubt Madge is Jules's mum, someone other than Malcolm must be her father."

Hetheridge started to reply, then stopped. His throat constricted. After a moment, he realized the thudding in his ears was his heartbeat.

"Chief?"

"Here," he mumbled.

"Don't take this as impertinence. But—I should tell you, from time to time, I dream about cases. Sometimes in the dreams, I notice things I miss while I'm awake. About a week ago, I dreamt I needed to interview Jules's father, and in the dream, he was ... Look. I'm wondering—what's your blood type?"

"B negative."

Silence. Then Kate said, "Who knows. Maybe it's a mistake, or just a coincidence. But if it's true ... I'm sorry I told you over the phone. I didn't want you to interview Madge and Jules without knowing, but I would have preferred to tell you face to face."

"Of course." Hetheridge defaulted into that cool courtesy, hammered into him from birth, which cost him no effort at all. "You have nothing to apologize for. My fault—I insisted you put me in the picture."

"Chief, I—"

"Hang on, someone needs me," he lied in that same bland tone. "Let me disconnect. I'll ring you back momentarily." Closing the phone, he held it against his chest as he stared, unseeing, toward the clouds of ground-creeping mist.

Hadn't they been careful? It was a long time ago, but he was always careful. Condoms, surely … until she assured him she was on the pill …

How soon after their breakup had she married Comfrey? Less than six months, or thereabout. At the time he'd received the news with relief. Madge had seemed so floored, so devastated when he'd ended the engagement, but she'd had no trouble bouncing back into a new relationship …

Or she'd been desperate to find one, Hetheridge thought, pulse still hammering in his ears. *Why didn't she tell me? Heaven knows I would have married her, made the best of it …*

It occurred to him that Madge might have wanted a husband who loved her for herself, not one who manfully accepted the sad necessity of commitment to her and her offspring. He wished he could recall what she'd said when he broke it off—how she'd looked, hints she might have given—but not even his excellent memory could dredge up that exchange. Because he'd paid more attention to himself, and to his feelings, than to hers.

Jules Comfrey. She might be his child. She was almost certainly his child.

Hetheridge closed his eyes, willing himself calm. Like any other man, he had tried to imagine what a son or daughter would be like, and the visions were pleasant and flattering. Never once had he envisioned a sullen, directionless young woman with a nightmare boyfriend and a drug habit or two.

Something came back to him then. It was his father in their family home, ensconced in a leather wingback chair, double old-fashioned in hand. It was the calm, measuring look, and the almost off-handed statement, "When I look at you, boy, I wonder how something like you ever came from me. Good God. What fools are men, to pin their hopes on sons."

Hetheridge felt himself go cold. He was under control. And the wiser half of his mind, the half he could depend on, told him exactly how to proceed. Reopening his phone, he rang Kate's mobile.

She picked up on the first ring. "Chief."

"Forgive the interruption. About Burt Rowland. Based on your interview, should he be placed under arrest?"

"No, I think he's clean. Clean of Ginny Rowland's death, at least."

"Fair enough. Caution him to remain in the city and release him. Make sure the scene is processed properly, then go home. We'll meet at nine o'clock tomorrow instead of seven. That should give you time to rest a bit before we compare notes. As you suggested, I'll send you out to interview Ivy Helgin. Now if DS Bhar is with you, put him on the line."

"I'm here, chief," Bhar said after a moment.

"Paul, I need you at the Yard as soon as possible. Madge and Jules Comfrey need to be re-interviewed, and I'd like you to handle it. I'm sure Kate told you why."

"I'll be right there." If Bhar was surprised, he gave no sign.

"One more thing. I believe both Madge and Jules are under the influence. I'm going to ask them to submit to drug tests right away. More than likely, both will refuse and demand their solicitor, and we'll be forced to compel them. But I'll make the attempt. See you when you arrive."

* * *

MADGE AND JULES were waiting inside New Scotland Yard's lobby alongside two uniformed constables. The room, cavernous and minimally lit, rang with a faint echo each time Madge took a step in her black patent heels. Noticing them for the first time, Hetheridge realized Madge had stormed a crime scene in those heels. Jules, at least, wore trainers and jeans. It was a generational difference, he supposed: Madge belonged to an era that still believed in dressing up to break the law.

Jules's agitation had not decreased. She was texting into her mobile while simultaneously pacing. Madge, if anything, looked asleep on her feet. Her pupils were tiny, and her arms were crossed over her chest.

"Escort Ms. Comfrey to an interview room. Mrs. Comfrey and I will talk in my office," Hetheridge told the constables.

"No way, you can't split us up," Jules cried, attention wrested from her phone at last. "Where Mum goes, I go."

Ignoring her, Hetheridge took Madge's arm and steered her toward the lifts. "Tell her to obey. I don't want this to turn into an arrest and an overnight stay," he said quietly.

"I'll be fine," Madge called to Jules in a weak voice. "Go with them, sweetheart. We're just here to talk. Don't be afraid."

Once the lift doors closed them in, Madge turned to Hetheridge. "You wouldn't actually arrest her, would you? She's not Kevin. She couldn't endure it."

"I'm within my rights to arrest her," Hetheridge said, noncommittal. "Why didn't you stop her from going to the Rowlands?"

Madge looked embarrassed. "I tried. But when one of Ginny's neighbors told us something was happening, and we called Burt's phone and couldn't get an answer, Jules went wild. She always loved Ginny and Burt, and she was afraid for them, that's all. When she wouldn't listen to me, and I couldn't convince her not to go, all I knew was to come along. I knew it was ridiculous, but I had no idea it was against so many laws."

The lift doors opened. Hetheridge led Madge to his office, unlocked the door and switched on the lights. Then without inviting her to sit or make herself comfortable, he said, "Tell me now. Is Jules my daughter?"

Madge's fuchsia-painted mouth worked. She made no sound, but her heavily lined eyes slid away from him, locking on something a few meters away. "I don't feel well. I need to sit down. Would you mind?"

He closed one hand over her right forearm, then another hand over her left, staring into her eyes. "Is Jules my daughter?"

Madge blinked at him. "Yes."

"What sort of drugs is she on?"

"Nothing," Madge cried. She struggled against his grip. "Let me go. Let me go, now, or I'll scream! You can't abuse me this way!"

Hetheridge released her in one motion. She staggered back, entirely from her own fear and lack of balance, yet staring at him in horror, as if he'd struck her.

"Tell me what drugs she's on."

"Nothing!" Madge cried. "Nothing! She's a good girl! And she's nothing to do with you. You're just the sperm donor. It's none of your business what she does, or doesn't do."

"I want you both to submit to urinalysis. Right now," Hetheridge said.

"No." Madge drew herself up. "Absolutely not! I demand my solicitor. And I demand you withdraw yourself from this case, Tony. Immediately!"

Before he knew what he would do, Hetheridge snatched away Madge's bag and dumped its contents on the dense green carpet. Keys ... a credit card case ... a pair of reading glasses ... a silver tube of lipstick ... a prescription bottle...

With a strangled cry, Madge dropped to her knees, reaching

for the prescription bottle. Hetheridge, far more limber despite the arthritis in his knee, was there first. Rising with the bottle in hand, he removed its cap and spilled the contents into his palm as Madge, still on her knees, stared up at him in outrage.

The bottle's label indicated thirty tablets of Valium for Madge Comfrey. And the Valium was there: small white round pills. But mixed in with them were larger yellow tablets, each stamped OC.

"Mixing Oxycontin with your Valium these days?"

"Give me that," Madge snapped, struggling to her feet. "You have no right! This is an illegal search—wait till I tell my solicitor!"

"Who gets these for you? Kevin?" Hetheridge asked. "Is that why you don't mind Jules seeing him? Because he has his uses for you, too?"

"Escort me downstairs now," Madge said, her voice like a glacier. "And pray to God, if you have a God other than yourself, that you still have a career once I'm done with you."

CHAPTER TWENTY-THREE

*O*hen Kate arrived at New Scotland Yard the next morning, she was in a mood that veered from cautiously optimistic to downright happy. The case was beginning to generate answers as well as questions. And she had a feeling—unsupported by logic, but strong, nevertheless—that Malcolm Comfrey's administrative assistant/mistress, Ivy Helgin, would hold the key to solving both murders. Was that why Kate felt an odd flutter in her stomach? The realization that her next interview might lead to an arrest, and then a conviction?

Or was it the prospect of seeing Hetheridge again?

Striding toward the bank of lifts, Kate caught a glance—an outright smirk—from a pinched-faced DC. Was that meant for her? Even if she had only two friends at the Yard, it was two more than she'd ever had before, and a measure of respect had accompanied the newfound companionship. The DC's smirk suggested Kate had devolved back into a pariah overnight.

Punching the lift's button, Kate glanced surreptitiously from left to right. Another glance, this time from DI Letty Marcum, a tall, broad-shouldered woman with a face as wide and flat as a shovel. The look, from DI Marcum's deep-set eyes, was aimed square at Kate, its message clear: You poor sod.

Geez, Kate thought, ashamed of how her heart sped up. *You'd think someone died.*

"Oi! Wakefield! Have a nice lie-in, did you?" came a jovial, overloud male voice behind her.

Kate turned to see Superintendent Jackson leering at her. He looked in a fine mood. A few other officers paused in their progress to observe the exchange.

The lift dinged behind her. Relieved, Kate spun toward it. "Sorry, gotta go ..."

"Leave it," Jackson said, his voice lifting high, as it did when he was angry or triumphant. "I've been waiting for you."

Kate felt a surge of suspicious dread. Jackson looked far too pleased. "Why?"

"You're mine, luv. Hetheridge's taken a powder. So you and Mahatma Ganges are back under my wing. We're going to solve the Comfrey and Rowland cases in record time and prove what a dream team we can be."

"What do you mean, Hetheridge's taken a powder?" Kate asked. Now her stomach wasn't fluttering, it was doing flips.

"Hetheridge is accused of brutalizing a witness and trying to force a confession. In fact, the witness, Mrs. Comfrey, is in the process of obtaining a restraining order against him. Commander Deaver tossed him off the case and called upon yours truly to pick up the pieces. Not surprising," Jackson grinned, "since the old man's arrest-conviction ratio is barely two-thirds of mine, and he's never been quick to wrap a major case."

That's because he only arrests people who are actually guilty, Kate tried to say. But at that moment, her stomach heaved, lava shot up her throat, and before Superintendent Jackson could jump aside, Kate vomited coffee and Blue Razz Berry Pop-Tarts all over his shoes.

* * *

BHAR WAS WAITING for Kate when she emerged from the ladies' lavatory more than a quarter-hour later. She knew she still looked pale and shell shocked, but a dab of lipstick and blush had somewhat reanimated her. This pregnancy-style vomiting reminded her of the time she'd eaten a bad bit of lobster—choking, heaving and spluttering long after every trace of sustenance was gone. Whenever she thought of Hetheridge's career in jeopardy, and Superintendent Jackson—Jackson!—taking his place, the purging started again. Finally, she forced herself to think of nothing but her desire to successfully interview Ivy Helgin. By keeping her mind focused on that goal, Kate calmed herself, washed her face and exited the lavatory with a semblance of dignity.

"You look like rubbish," Bhar said.

"And you look manic. Like you chewed coffee beans all night and washed them down with Red Bull."

"I'm planning on murdering Jackson," Bhar said conversationally. "Every detective has his own murder plan. Mine is flawless—no DNA or dental evidence left behind. Just you wait. You'll know I did it, but you'll never work out how."

"What happened to the chief last night?" Kate's left side still ached. She pressed a hand against it, ignoring the curious glances from those passing through the corridor.

"I don't know," Bhar admitted. "Supposedly he took Madge Comfrey up to his office, slapped her around, searched her person and tried to coerce a confession. Madge and her daughter were baying at the moon when I got here, playing it up for their solicitor and threatening to bring down the Met. I did the only thing I could think of."

Kate waited.

"I arrested them. Because the crime is murder, we have thirty-six hours to hold them before we have to officially charge them with anything."

Kate let out her breath all at once. "Bold move."

"They bloody well deserved it." Bhar was unrepentant. "Think there's any chance Hetheridge brutalized Madge?"

"None."

"Right. So a night in lockup was just what those lying harpies deserved. They refused all questions on advice of their solicitor, by the way. So I stayed up all night and still have sod-all new information—well, except for their drug tests, which were positive. Mum does downers and painkillers. Little Miss does coke. But because of who they are, Jackson isn't about to prosecute them for what amounts to minor indiscretions. And to be honest, I doubt Hetheridge would have bothered with vice charges, either. God, I'm tired." Pressing his palms to his eyes, Bhar yawned mightily, then looked Kate over with something more akin to his usual good-natured expression. "So what gives with you? I know Jackson revolts you even more than he revolts me, but puking all over his Oxfam shoes seems over the top. You're not in the club, are you?"

Kate sighed.

Bhar's eyes went wide. "You're kidding? You are?" He stared at her for several seconds, then leaned close and whispered, "Is it the chief's?"

Groaning, Kate pushed him back. "Of course not. Do the maths. And never mind that now. Can I assume the super's waiting for us?"

"He is. Let us go and hearken to the world's greatest detective."

* * *

WHEN THEY ENTERED Superintendent Jackson's office, the gang

was assembled—two junior DCs, two detective sergeants and three DIs who fluctuated between one super's team and another, depending on need. Clearly, Commander Deaver had grown weary of the Comfrey-Rowland case, and was willing to provide the manpower to resolve it as soon as possible.

Superintendent Jackson, who fancied himself both an over-powering authority figure and a regular bloke, sat man-of-the-people style in the center of the room. The remains of a jam doughnut was in his right hand—the empty box, stained with red goo, lay open on the desk beside him.

"No, no, listen to this one," he cried over a shout of laughter. "What about an all-girl threesome? Whaddya call that?"

"Ménage a twat," Kate said. She'd heard it around the Yard at least half a dozen times.

Jackson pressed the doughnut into his mouth and chewed, studying her as the room went silent. "Watch out, boys," he said at last, around a mouthful of cake and jam. "The headmistress will castrate you if you step out of line."

Kate put on a game smile and shrugged. She had chosen her place in what was still a man's world. There was a time to assert her equality, and a time to let deliberate provocation slide.

"Done sicking up?" Jackson continued. "Better watch it, Wakefield. Folks will say you're in the club."

"No way," Kate lied, keeping that I-know-how-to-take-my-lumps expression on her face. "A shock to hear Hetheridge was out and I'd been reassigned again, that's all. But now I'm here, I promise to do my best, sir."

"As do I," Bhar muttered, somewhat less convincingly.

"Well." Jackson folded his arms across his chest. "While we were waiting on you and the boy wonder to turn up, we were discussing errors in the Comfrey-Rowland investigation."

"Really?" Bhar asked in a cold voice, before Kate could inter-vene with another simpering reply. "Enlighten us."

"First, the obvious: breaking the law. Coercing a confession is a shocking lapse." Jackson clucked to his audience. "Second: dismissing material evidence. The balcony window was open, was it not? The inside garage door had been forced. Two clear signs that the killer broke into the house, as I believe the crime scene photos also indicate.

"Third," Jackson said, rising and staring not at Kate, but at Bhar. "Allowing a pair of, shall we say, 'inexperienced' detectives to flit from theory to theory, antagonizing witnesses in the process. A successful investigation begins with a vision and follows that vision right down to arrest, trial and conviction."

"You've read the reports," Bhar said before Kate could stop him. "Tell us who you've decided is guilty and we'll manufacture the evidence to prove it. Sir."

Jackson's face split in a triumphant grin. "No. You're used to having your head, Bhar. You tell me what your next move would be."

Anything but the truth, Kate thought. But, as she feared, Bhar's desire to be proven right outweighed his wisdom in dealing with Jackson.

"I think it's time we discovered exactly how much Madge and Jules Comfrey stood to inherit on Malcolm Comfrey's death," Bhar said. "I'd also like to discover if their drug abuse is new, or part of a long-standing pattern."

"Wrong," Jackson said. "Faulty programming. Don't let it get you down, mate. Your correct answer would be, research previous break-ins around the Comfreys' neighborhood in the last eighteen months. That's the route which will lead to resolution."

"Research?"

"Research," Jackson declared, unable to hide his pleasure at Bhar's indignation. "Research and a report on my desk by five this evening. Or the Commander and I will have a discussion about your ability to play well with others." He turned to

Kate. "What about you? What should your next assignment be?"

"I'm a little uncertain," she lied. "Last night, I found out Malcolm Comfrey had a mistress named Ivy Helgin. She was also his administrative assistant. And you know what they say about no stone unturned. So I thought interviewing Miss Helgin might be a good idea. As Comfrey's assistant, she would know if he'd received death threats at the office. Or if he feared some enemy from his business dealings might seek him out at home ..."

That last bit struck a chord with Jackson's predetermined scenario. He gave Kate a benevolent smile.

"Good. Good!" He glanced around the silent faces to emphasize his approval. "Never let it be said I won't admit it when one of you hits the right scent. Find and interview this Ivy Helgin, Kate. Pay special attention to any worries or concerns Comfrey expressed during his last days. Who knows? Perhaps you'll unearth something that pertains to the murder."

Kate, not daring to meet Bhar's incredulous stare, forced a self-effacing smile. "Thank you, sir. I'll get right on it."

* * *

OUTSIDE OF NEW SCOTLAND YARD, stomach still twisting ominously, Kate made several phone calls. The first, to Ivy Helgin's directory number, was successful. Ms. Helgin answered, expressed a desire to cooperate with the investigation, and agreed to meet Kate for lunch in Piccadilly Circus at one o'clock.

Her second call, to Hetheridge's mobile, was met only by rings and an invitation to leave a message. On the third attempt she did, saying only, "Tony. Paul and I are thinking of you. We'll ring again later."

Her third call was more problematic. The number was ex-directory, so Kate was forced to use the Met's resources to gain the information. Then she had to convince a Jamaican-born housekeeper her need to speak with the mistress was legitimate. By the time the person in question came on the line, Kate had spent twenty minutes trying to reach her.

"Lady Margaret," she said, "it's DS Kate Wakefield. I'm sorry to disturb you. But I need your help."

CHAPTER TWENTY-FOUR

*I*vy Helgin pushed bits of her duck confit, a dish the Criterion Grill was known for doing well, around her plate. She looked as if her appetite had fled. Kate, who found the expensive mess's aroma nauseating, avoided looking at the other woman's plate. She herself had ordered mineral water and a bowl of thin soup, but managed to swallow only a few mouthfuls of either.

"I haven't enjoyed much since Mal died." Sighing, Ivy put an elbow on the table and plopped her chin on her palm, like a bored child. "I've never grieved before. Never lost anyone before Mal."

That came as little surprise to Kate. It wasn't just Ivy's youth —she was twenty-four—that made a history of serial mourning unlikely. It was her wide green eyes, her infectious smile, the lack of lines on her forehead, and even the way her strawberry-blond hair rippled to her shoulders in flawless, symmetric waves. Ivy Helgin seemed to be one of life's chosen few: a good soul reared by good souls, properly nourished and educated, treated kindly at every turn and beaming that same kindness back into the world, with the innocence of a creature who knows nothing else.

After twenty minutes with Ivy, who carried herself like a duchess and addressed doormen, waiters and a detective sergeant from New Scotland Yard like a long-lost friend, Kate had to struggle to keep her jealousy in check.

"How long were you with him?" Kate asked.

"Two years," Ivy said. "My first real job. I came on as the junior assistant to Miss Greggor, who'd been with Mal since he founded the company. Six months in, she retired and I began working with him more closely. I wasn't the best assistant," Ivy admitted with a charming, self-deprecating laugh. "I muddled lots of things, especially maths. Sometimes Mal had to tutor me. But it was wonderful spending so much time in his company. Those first few weeks after Miss Greggor left, I began to know the real Mal, and it was wonderful." She smiled at Kate, her eyes bright with memory.

"Didn't bother you that he was married?" Kate didn't succeed in sounding neutral. Some shriveled part of her wanted to shame Ivy, to wipe that smile off the younger woman's face.

"Oh, it bothered me a great deal," Ivy said, still pushing duck confit here and there. "And I didn't dare discuss it with my parents, or Father Vernon. It's not that I worried about their disapproval. I just didn't want to put them through the pain of feeling disappointed in me. And to be fair, Mal's situation wasn't the typical one, of a straying husband out for what he could get. I couldn't subject his conduct to the judgment of those who wouldn't understand."

Kate forced herself to take another sip of water. Her left side still ached, and she suspected dehydration was as much the culprit as that morning's violent retching. "So in what way was Malcolm Comfrey's marital situation atypical?"

"Well, his wife had drawn a line in the sand. She wanted to remain married only for the sake of their daughter, and their social standing. Mal agreed because he was a gentleman who believed in the sanctity of marriage. But he was only human," Ivy said. "He hadn't been allowed to experience love or passion in years. He was starving for affection. And I ..." Breaking off, Ivy shook her head, pausing to master herself. "I believe we were fated to meet. I believe when two people share such a deep love, there can be no sin. It's meant to be. It's destiny."

"I don't know if Mrs. Comfrey would agree with the in-name-only characterization of her marriage to Mr. Comfrey," Kate said, striving to keep the cynicism from her voice. No sense alienating a witness so unguarded. "Did you observe some interaction between them that convinced you Mrs. Comfrey agreed to her husband arranging an alternate relationship? How did she get on with you, for example?"

Putting down her fork at last, Ivy covered her plate with her linen napkin. "Mrs. Comfrey treated me with a sort of cool courtesy. Nothing more. Nothing less. And I didn't push. I thought it might be somewhat hard for her, to see her husband—even though she had rejected him—with a much younger woman. So I tried to be discreet and professional in her presence. As if Mal and I were nothing but business associates."

Recalling Ginny Rowland's belief that Ivy was too attractive, sharp and upwardly mobile to accept a man like Comfrey unless marriage were on the table, Kate asked, "Didn't it bother you that Mr. Comfrey couldn't offer you marriage?"

"Oh, you have it wrong. For the last few months, we were engaged," Ivy said, surprised. "Want to see the ring?"

The waiter, a rotund man with a natural tonsure, chose that moment to appear. Before Kate could retrieve her jaw from the floor, he scooped up Ivy's rejected plate and Kate's nearly untouched soup.

"Can I offer you anything more?"

"I'd like to be bad," Ivy confided to the waiter, then shot a glance at Kate. "What do you think? Want to be bad this once?"

Kate shrugged.

Ivy turned back to the waiter. She gave him that smile again, a smile which expected all the world to return her good will, since it had never failed her yet. And to Kate's amazement, the working stiff visibly thawed.

"What do you have," Ivy asked, "that's really, really bad?"

"We have crème brûlée," the waiter said. "But the molten volcano cake is much worse. A small chocolate Bundt, filled with brandy-laced fudge, set afire. To die for," he concluded, enjoying the excitement in Ivy's eyes.

"We'll take two!" Ivy squealed.

"I can't have anything brandy-laced," Kate said. "Pregnant."

"Crème brûlée for you, then," Ivy said. Nodding, the waiter hurried off to place the order.

Kate, motivated by frugality rather than actual need, muttered, "I didn't get a look at the prices …"

"Oh, don't worry, detective, this is on me," Ivy said, her kindness too unforced to be anything but genuine. "My little sideline business has succeeded beyond my wildest dreams. I've had to hire an accountant and a personal assistant just to keep up. So treating you is my pleasure. But I mentioned the ring …" She dug in her bag, producing a burgundy velvet box. Opening it, she removed a ring and put it on.

"Beautiful, isn't it?" She extended her hand to Kate.

Kate stared at the ring. A bright center diamond of at least two carats was set in platinum or white gold. Clustered around that center stone, smaller canary diamonds were arranged alongside bright red rubies. On Ivy's hand, the ring blazed, impossible to ignore—the cold purity of a diamond encircled by both light and heat.

"Good grief," Kate breathed, forgetting her manners. "What's it worth? Oh, sorry," she amended, mortified. "That slipped out. It's gorgeous."

Ivy nodded. As she stared at the ring, her eyes began to shine. After a moment, she wiped at them, twisted the ring off her finger, and replaced it in the box, closing the burgundy-furred lid with a snap.

"I'd prefer to wear it always," she told Kate, tucking the ring box back in her bag. "But not until this investigation into Mal's death ends. I wouldn't want to risk Mrs. Comfrey seeing it and understanding it came from her husband. I have it. I know what it meant. I don't have to flaunt it to the whole world."

Kate digested this information while Ivy sniffed, wiped her eyes and used the silence to compose herself. Before their conversation resumed, the waiter reappeared, this time with a lump of dark chocolate debauchery for Ivy, and a virginal white ramekin for Kate.

Accepting a small torch from an assistant, the waiter passed the flame over Ivy's cake, which erupted into blue flame. Ivy squealed, clapping. Patrons at nearby tables seconded her delight with laughter and an additional spatter of applause. When the fire disappeared, the waiter turned to Kate's ramekin. Passing the blue flame over the top of the dessert, he moved it from side to side until the top was caramelized. Kate found the sugary odor disgusting, and no one applauded the result. Switching off the torch, the waiter turned back to Ivy, offered his sincere wish that she would enjoy the dessert, and bustled away.

"You mentioned your little side business." Kate ignored her crème brûlée as Ivy tucked into her molten volcano cake. "I thought you were Malcolm Comfrey's administrative assistant. You have another business, too?"

Ivy savored a mouthful of chocolate, moaned in delight, then managed to answer. "Oh, yes, I was still Mal's assistant, even after we became engaged. But not as much hands-on, you see. I actually had a junior assistant, Harriet, and she was absolutely brill. In the end, she took on most of Mal's heavy lifting—she'd had special courses to prepare herself for that sort of work, you see—while I kept Mal happy and brainstormed new ideas for my business. Dino-Vits!"

"Dino-Vits?" Kate repeated. To be polite, she broke into the crème brûlée with her dessert fork's delicate tines, but did not attempt to swallow a piece.

"Yes. The idea came to me one night while in bed. With Mal," Ivy whispered, a pretty blush appearing on her cheeks. "We were talking about what the world needs most. Of course, I said the world's most important resource is children, because children are the future. And it's a tragedy that so many of them live in poverty. And Malcolm said when you're in poverty, you have to pull yourself up by your bootstraps. And I said no, too many children don't have boots, and they don't have strength. They don't have the good nutrition, for one thing, to become strong. They don't have the vitamins and minerals we take for granted. So suddenly I had this idea of giving every child in the world a free supply of vitamins. So they can grow up strong and pull themselves out of poverty!"

Kate tossed her linen napkin atop the crème brûlée. "Sorry. Sudden nausea. Pay no attention to me, pregnancy does funny things to your body. So what did Mr. Comfrey think of your idea to distribute free vitamins to the world's poor?"

"Well, at first he laughed at me, and was rude," Ivy admitted, pausing between phrases to enjoy her molten cake. "Then he had a change of heart, and said he would give me a stake to start the business. I couldn't give away the vitamins for free, but I could offer them at the most competitive rates in the entire world." Ivy grinned at Kate. "Of course, I was over the moon. I decided to call the product Dino-Vits because all children everywhere adore dinosaurs. And we manufactured the vitamin pills to be chewable and even shaped like the three best dinosaurs: T. rex, velociraptor and apatosaurus."

"And this business is a success?"

"An unprecedented success!" Ivy said. "It's like, the moment I put the idea out to the universe, the universe responded with money! Dino-Vits got investors right away. I think Mal must have done a lot of lobbying for me behind closed doors. But the outpouring of response was amazing. And believe it or not, it's made me rich," she said, dropping back into a whisper. "I bought my parents a new home. Paid off my sister's debts. I could retire right now and never work again in my life. All from the first six months of the business. I reckon being a good person really does pay in the end."

Kate studied Ivy for a long moment. Something Burt Rowland said occurred to her as she watched the younger woman finish her cake. When the dessert was nothing but a brown smear across the gold-edged plate, Kate asked, "How's the Dino-Vits business done since Malcolm Comfrey died?"

Ivy blinked. "Actually, it's lost money for the first time ever. I'm supposed to meet with my accountant next week. That's why I think Mal must have been helping me somehow, behind the scenes. All the contracts and orders are still in place, but the remittances have slowed to almost nothing."

Kate nodded. "Back to your engagement. Did you and Mr. Comfrey actually set a date?"

"No." Ivy shook her head. "He said first, he had to tell his wife their life together was over."

* * *

BACK IN HER CAR, Kate checked her smart phone for messages. Nothing from Hetheridge or Bhar. But Lady Margaret had called, and Kate wasted no time ringing her back. When Lady Margaret came on the line, her information was everything an investigator could hope for: first-hand, succinct and germane. As Lady Margaret spoke in her crisp, no-nonsense tone, Kate sat behind the wheel and nodded, smiling idiotically as foot traffic passed her vehicle on both sides. Inside her head, the pieces were locking into place, one after another.

"Thank you, Lady Margaret," she breathed before disconnecting. She sat for another moment, still aware of her dodgy stomach and aching side, but no longer concerned with them. She knew. She was sure she knew. Now to call Hetheridge.

Her phone trilled. Startled, Kate glanced at it, expecting to see Hetheridge's name on the screen. Instead, she saw one of the Yard's endless permutations of internal lines. That meant it was probably Jackson, or Bhar.

"Wakefield," she answered warily.

"It's me. Dead man working," Bhar sighed in her ear. "You're recalled to the Yard. The case has broken. We're making an arrest."

"What do you mean?"

"The 9 millimeter gun that killed Ginny Rowland came back covered with prints. Charlie Fringate's prints. Remember his prior conviction? Easy match for SO4. Jackson's thrilled. The whole intruder-burglar angle has been dropped and it's Fringate all the way. He was reputedly carrying on with Madge Comfrey. So as the theory goes, he killed her husband to get him out of the way—and when Ginny Rowland threatened him with blackmail, and he was facing another bankruptcy and couldn't afford to pay, he killed her, too."

Kate sighed. "I have to give Jackson credit, that makes more sense than most of the conclusions he leaps to. But it's still wrong. How does he explain that Fringate supposedly had the wit to wipe down the fire iron after beating Comfrey to a pulp, yet when he shot Ginny Rowland in the back, he somehow forgot to wipe his prints off the gun?"

Bhar was silent for a moment. "Kate. Geez. I didn't even ask myself that."

"That's because you're asleep on your feet. Listen, the last time Jackson went down the wrong road, I faced him directly and lost, and an innocent person went to trial. I won't risk that happening again. Tell Jackson you couldn't get me to answer my phone."

"He'll find that hard to believe. Forensic should be calling you soon, too. Remember when the chief told Knestrick to check all the dustbins in the neighborhood, not just the Comfreys'? It's taken Knestrick this long to examine them, but in one of the bins he struck pay dirt. A heap of billion thread count bath towels soaked with blood. No doubt the majority is Malcolm Comfrey's. With any luck, traces of the killer's DNA will be on them, too. If Fringate's innocent, he'll get off. Still want to risk Jackson's wrath?"

"I just need an hour or two. Just long enough to re-interview the person who actually killed Malcolm Comfrey and Ginny Rowland."

"Who?" Bhar demanded.

"Madge Comfrey," Kate said. "I know she did it. And I think I know why."

CHAPTER TWENTY-FIVE

ate almost made the mistake of heading toward the hotel where she had interviewed the Comfreys twice before—an error that could have burned up an hour in London traffic. Then she recalled Superintendent Jackson's typical method of dealing with the affluent—grand gestures and obsequiousness. If Hetheridge had been perceived as offensive to Madge Comfrey, Jackson would seek to advance his own cause by giving Madge proof of his good will. He would declare the CID investigation of the Comfrey house finished, and allow the Comfreys to return home. A quick call to the Yard confirmed it, and Kate turned her vehicle toward Belgravia.

In the Comfreys' pea-graveled car park, Kate switched off her smart phone's ringer, putting the device in journal mode. To assure a smooth prosecution, she needed to document everything Madge Comfrey said. To her surprise, Kate didn't feel especially nervous as she approached the front entrance's tall columns and red-lacquered double doors. Her hands were steady, her heartbeat, only slightly elevated. She had been trained for this; she had served her apprenticeship as the second or third officer on a dozen other arrests. She was prepared to take the lead.

Chimes sounded within the house when Kate pressed the doorbell. What felt like a full minute passed. Just as Kate was ready to mash the button again, she heard the tap of heels against marble, and Madge Comfrey opened the door.

Madge's brown hair was still arranged in that stiff halo of perfect waves. She wore a loose frock, probably Laura Ashley, with a dense floral print. Her preprogrammed expression of welcome shifted to contempt when she recognized Kate.

"Good afternoon, Detective. I assume you've come to issue another apology on your superior's behalf. Write a letter, if you feel you must." Madge moved to close the door in Kate's face.

"Nope," Kate said, interposing herself between door and jamb with her left shoulder. "You have my sincere regrets for any mistreatment you may have suffered, Mrs. Comfrey. But the case isn't closed yet. There are loose ends to be wrapped up, and we need your help."

Madge's fingers tightened on the brass door handle, as if she contemplated shoving Kate backward and slamming the door. "What sort of loose ends?"

"May I come in?" Kate's tone was polite.

"I'd prefer not."

"Very well." Kate removed her smart phone's stylus. "I'm not sure what your neighbors will make of me interviewing you on your doorstep, but let's hope they keep their speculations to themselves, rather than call the media."

Madge's silver-frosted eyelids narrowed. Opening the door wide, she indicated the foyer. "Do come in."

The stink of lemon furniture polish hung in the air. As Kate followed Madge into the parlor where she and Hetheridge had conducted that first interview, the odor intensified. Although Madge had been home fewer than twenty-four hours, a frenzy of cleaning and depersonalization was underway. The oil painting over the mantle had been removed; the framed photographs were gone; all the small touches Kate remembered from the night of the first murder, like that bowl of yellow chrysanthemums, had disappeared. The room was being transformed into the blank canvas only a prospective buyer could love.

"I heard you were putting the house up for sale," Kate said. "Arranging for a major estate auction, too."

"Where did you ...?" Madge cut off her own question. "Of course. Lady Margaret Knolls. When that nosy parker calls offering sympathy, she's only trawling for gossip. And I thought I was being clever, enlisting her suggestions for the proper estate agent to wring the most out of the sale, since she associates with those wretched creatures."

"The only form of life lower than a copper is an estate agent," Kate agreed, smiling at Madge and wondering if she might actually forge a connection with her. "It couldn't have been easy to learn your husband died whilst in bankruptcy proceedings, and you and Jules stood to inherit very little. Just this house and its contents, once the agent tallies up the value."

"I don't know what you're talking about." Straightening her back, Madge put on the upper-middle class hauteur Kate despised to the depths of her working-class soul. "Perhaps people of your background habitually indulge in such vulgar discussions. People of mine do not. If you have a legitimate question pertaining to my late husband's death, please ask it."

Goaded, Kate shot back without thinking, "Did you beat him to death because he loved Ivy Helgin? Or because he transferred all his assets to her? Meaning you and Jules would be forced to earn your living, like the rest of the planet?"

Madge's fuchsia lips twisted into a sneer. Was that vindictive expression the last thing Malcolm Comfrey and Ginny Rowland had ever seen?

As if she'd plucked the latter name from Kate's mind, Madge said, "Moments like these, I rather wish Ginny were still alive. We used to have a bit of fun, psychoanalyzing the motives of creatures like Ivy. And you, come to that. How you quite likely embarked on a career in law enforcement for the opportunity to harass your betters without fear of retribution. I'm glad you're the one who came to question me. Now I can continue the analysis, even if Ginny's no longer able to compare notes."

Turning to the liquor trolley beside the long white sofa, Madge poured herself a glass of brandy. Unselfconscious, she swallowed half of it at a gulp, as if Kate were a tradesperson or some other nonentity. Then her head swiveled back to Kate, her smile a parody of the gracious hostess. "Do you take your gin straight, or submerged in fizzy soda?"

Kate let it go. She was determined not to lose her self-control again. "You discovered your husband was illegally liquidating his own business, didn't you, Mrs. Comfrey?"

"He boasted of it." Madge sneered again. "You wouldn't believe a man impotent for ten years could think with his dick, but such is the miracle of Viagra. Oh, yes, he was rapturously in love with Ivy, taking our life savings—the millions he could never have earned without me by his side—and concealing it in her ludicrous vitamin company. Quite a nest egg for their future wedded life. I must say, Ginny and I had a laugh at the notion of Ivy setting up house for Mal. Fitted carpet in every room, three-piece suites of furniture, and a print of Monet's *Water Lilies* in a 'living room,' no doubt. You've been personal with me, Detective, so I'll be personal with you. Does it follow, to your sort's way of thinking, that once you've married up, you'll be welcomed as a member of the new class? That your husband's old friends will teach you how to dress, speak, entertain and so on, without continually giving offense?"

"You tell me. Didn't you try to move up the ladder by marrying Tony Hetheridge? Didn't Ginny Rowland go from prostitute to financier's wife?"

"Ah, but Ginny was brilliant at transformation. Too damned smart for her own good, if you ask me," Madge added with a chuckle.

Recognizing the germ of a confession within that sound, Kate's skin prickled into gooseflesh. There was something hypnotically cobra-like in Madge's manner, in how she alluded to murder in those plummy tones, as if Kate were the one who ought to be ashamed of herself. Was that why Kate still hovered beside the cold hearth, too intimidated to sit down without invitation, neglecting even to take notes? Without Hetheridge's presence to span the class abyss, was she incapable of seizing control?

A faint noise, like a door closing at the back of the house, startled Kate. Madge, refilling her glass, didn't seem to notice. Perhaps the Comfreys' cleaner was still rattling around the place, boxing up whatnots before the estate agent arrived?

"I like how you call your superior 'Tony.'" Madge saw Kate open her mouth to speak, but cut across her without a flicker of apology. "Ginny told me she teased him about you and that other detective, the blackie, and Tony came over all baronial. Huffed he was Lord Hetheridge, thank you very much, and not to be mocked. It amuses Tony to play the egalitarian, but make no mistake—he's nearly as complete a rotter as Malcolm ever was. The only difference between the aristocracy and Mal's sort is, the aristocrats prize blood above all. They never turn on their own."

"So that's why you killed Mr. Comfrey?" This time, Kate interrupted Madge, East London accent escaping. "Because he turned on you and Jules? Except, of course, he couldn't really count Jules as blood, could he? Not when she's CS Hetheridge's daughter."

"I have Ginny to thank for Mal hearing of that." Madge looked almost sad. "Smart as she was, Ginny was greedy, too. She resorted to blackmail—first with Mal, then with me. That's why our friendship ended on a cool note."

Such masterful understatement would usually force at least a grudging smile from Kate. But she was stung too deeply by Madge's barbs to do anything but accuse in a monotone, "So you shot her in the back."

"Couldn't manage it any other way," Madge admitted with brittle good humor. "Quite different with Mal, I assure you. With him, it wasn't about extortion, or keeping out of prison. It was about beating that bloody triumphant look off his face.

"He never got out of his chair, you know," Madge went on, describing her victim's behavior as another Belgravia housewife might recount a shop girl's abominable cheek. "Just put aside his book and told me his plans. He was so proud of scheming up a way to cast me off, marry Ivy and leave Jules and me with nothing but crumbs.

"I demanded to know why. He said I was old." Madge's lips compressed into a dangerous slash. "As if he wasn't! And he said things about Jules so heartless, they made my skin crawl. He went on and on, doing what he loved best to someone he no longer loved at all."

A second door opened somewhere, the sound of a voice, a scrape and a thump. What if the cleaner popped in to say her goodbyes, prompting Madge to recall herself and demand a solicitor? Moments ago, Kate would have cursed an interruption. Now something in Madge's war paint, in the mad light of her pale blue eyes, made Kate almost wish someone would wander in.

"Maybe you just meant to threaten your husband, and things got out of hand?" Kate offered, eyes on the parlor door. "Maybe you didn't mean to kill him?"

"I meant to walk away." Madge downed another gulp of brandy. "That's what he couldn't endure. He called me back, like a headmaster summoning a schoolboy. When he finished dressing me down, I was ill. Violently ill, heaving up my guts while he laughed."

"Mum!" It was Jules. Madge didn't answer, didn't even seem to hear, still holding Kate's gaze with increasing intensity.

"When I composed myself, Malcolm said he'd pack his bags in the morning. In the meantime, he'd finish his drink. 'The fire's dying,' he said. He pointed to the fireplace and said, 'Stir it up before you go.'"

"Mum!" Jules called again, louder.

"Oi! Madge!" Kevin shouted. Raucous laughter followed.

"I never felt out of control," Madge continued defiantly, as if Kate counted on such an excuse. "Just done with him. Done with Malcolm Comfrey taking up space on this earth. So I stirred up the fire and hit him with the poker until my arm ached, until his blood stuck to my face and hair. Then I drove the poker into his skull. He was still alive. Gurgled a bit, with the poker hanging out of his eye socket. I watched him die. And felt nothing. Everything. But not sorry."

"Mum!" The door banged open as Jules bounded into the parlor. "Kevin and I are starving! Want us to bring you back a takeaway curry?"

Jules wore her KEVIN'S TOY T-shirt and ripped blue jeans. Her resemblance to Hetheridge was obvious, now that Kate expected it, despite the girl's dilated pupils and loopy grin. Kevin Whitley, appearing at Jules's shoulder, also looked in the grip of some marvelous diversion.

Jules recognized Kate. The girl's features, briefly happy, reassumed their natural sullen look. "What's she doing here, Mum? Aren't we suing Scotland Yard?"

"Was it Jules who helped conceal your guilt?" Kate prodded Madge. "Or was it Kevin?"

That contemptuous curl of the lips again, that mad light in the eyes. "They're innocent, Detective. Haven't you been listening?"

"What's she on about?" Kevin demanded of Kate.

"Mrs. Comfrey told me she killed her husband. I want to know how she concealed the evidence."

Jules made a high-pitched noise of denial. Kevin, more practical despite his drug du jour, was outraged. "She can't do this to you, Madge. Call a solicitor! Don't say nothing else!"

Madge shook her head. Swallowing the remains of her drink,

she set the glass back on the liquor trolley with a thump of finality.

"I don't need a solicitor." Madge reached into the front pocket of her dress, withdrawing a black snub-nosed pistol. "I have everything under control."

"Hang on!" Kevin cried. "That's mine!"

Kate's throat constricted as her stomach gave a steep, sickening lurch. As Madge braced her right hand with her left, keeping the gun level, Kate heard something small and metallic clatter to the floor. Her smart phone had fallen—because her fingers had forgotten to clasp it.

"Watch it, Detective. I was shaky with Ginny. Won't be shaky with you."

"Mum!" Jules cried.

"M-Mrs. Comfrey," Kate said, horrified at how her voice shook and determined to speak regardless. "Put down the gun. You won't commit a third murder right in front of your daughter."

Madge spared trembling, white-faced Jules a glance. "You're nothing to her," she said, locking gazes with Kate again. "And she needn't look. It'll all be done in the blink of an eye."

"Mum, I don't care if you killed Dad!" Jules darted close to Madge, almost close enough to shield Kate from the gun barrel. "I'm glad you did! He deserved it. But you didn't kill Ginny. You couldn't have."

"I never killed your father, darling. I should have told you long ago—you were Malcolm's in name only." The gun wavered as Madge took on a wheedling tone. "As for Ginny—I would have fixed things differently, I promise. I only took along Charlie's shooter for self-defense. But she'd guessed about Malcolm, and said if I didn't pay up, she'd sell the story to the tabloids. I had no choice."

"In name only?" Jules repeated, eyes brimming with tears.

Hope surged in Kate. If Jules rushed to her mother, blocking

Madge's aim, it could provide Kate's only chance to escape. But even as Kate prepared to run, Kevin pushed Jules aside, lunging for the pistol.

"Give me that!"

The gun went off. Kate's ears rang and she tasted bile. But she managed to keep her feet, even as Jules dropped to her knees with a wail and Kevin blundered into the liquor trolley, sending it crashing to the floor. Only Madge remained calm, bracing her right hand as she again trained the weapon on Kate.

"That's mine," Kevin howled again, kicking himself free of the liquor trolley with another loud crash. "You stole it, you mad bat!"

Kate tore her gaze from the gun long enough to glance at Jules. The girl was back on her feet, fists pressed against her mouth to hold in the sobs, but physically unharmed. No bullet hole marred any of the walls Kate could see—which meant it was probably lodged in the plaster behind her head.

Jules's half-muffled sobs escalated in pitch. "Oh, for God's sake, darling, go," Madge snapped. "No one will ever be able to prove you witnessed this. I'll be in touch once I reach the Continent. I mean it, Kev!" she said louder, when he seemed poised to lunge for his weapon again. "Take Jules and go!"

"If you want to help Mrs. Comfrey, one of you should stay here," Kate said, fighting to keep her voice steady. "The other should call 999 ..."

"Oh, come off it." Madge took a step toward Kate, lifting the pistol and cocking the hammer.

Jules, face blotchy and eyes red, took a last look at Kate over her shoulder. Then Kevin pulled her through the doorway, and they were gone.

"Killing me won't change things for you." The words tumbled out as Kate realized neither Jules nor Kevin would call anyone on her behalf. "And murdering a police officer will destroy any hope of a light sentence."

"I won't get a light sentence. I'll get life. Besides, you underestimate me," Madge smiled. "When it comes to killing, I seem to be a gifted amateur. All my life, I've been a good girl. Even when His Lordship pushed me aside, did I force him to pay me off or marry me? No. I found another man to provide the only thing I ever wanted—security. If Malcolm hadn't tried to deny me what was mine, I would have let him go. As it was, I quite enjoyed taking his life. Perhaps I'll enjoy taking yours, too."

"Not as much as you'd enjoy taking mine, Madge. Let Sergeant Wakefield go. It's me you have a grudge against."

Kate didn't dare turn, but she would have known that voice anywhere.

"Let the sergeant go. Let me take her place," Hetheridge said. "Madge, I'm making you a serious offer."

"Why would I do that?"

"She has no history with you. She's done nothing to harm you. You and I are the ones with unfinished business."

For the first time, Madge looked uncertain. "Why bargain? I have five bullets. I could shoot you both."

"One of us would make it across the room before the second shot," Hetheridge said. "You'll lose control if you get greedy, Madge."

"Are you lecturing me again?" Madge's voice trembled with anger. "That's why I mix painkillers with my Valium. Because men have treated me like rubbish all my life. That's why I kept Jules from you, Tony. Because I never wanted her father to reject her as heartlessly as he rejected me, once the novelty of her existence wore off."

"Madge." Kate heard Hetheridge take a measured step forward. "I'm sorry for what I did to you. Truly sorry. Let Sergeant Wakefield go."

"Come closer," Madge said.

Hetheridge took one step past Kate, then another. He did not look at her. He came to a halt less than a meter from the gun, which Madge pointed at his face.

"You can go," Madge said to Kate, her eyes on Hetheridge.

Kate couldn't move. She didn't want to. All she could do, even in the grip of terror, was try and calculate some superhuman way she could reach the gun and wrestle it away before Madge could pull the trigger.

"Go," Hetheridge said.

Kate couldn't make herself move.

"Go now!" Hetheridge roared.

Kate's body responded quicker than her brain. First she was stumbling, then running, escaping the house the way she'd come. Bursting out of the double doors, she hit the front steps, falling into the arms of Paul Bhar. Superintendent Jackson's second unit had set up camp on the Comfreys' front lawn. A van-based command center was parked on the street while several panda cars, blue lights flashing, were positioned to impede traffic.

"Couldn't let you do this alone," Paul said, holding Kate tight. "I called Tony, and he called out the troops. Then he insisted on going in, through that broken side door. Are you all right?"

Kate tried to answer, but no sound came from her—just the thunderous boom of a gunshot inside the house.

Pulling away from Paul, Kate surged toward the red-lacquered doors, powered by terror and no thought except to get to Hetheridge. Hands caught her, seizing her shoulders and waist. She kicked and flailed, screaming for release, but they didn't let go.

A deadly shift occurred around Kate. It was the slide and pop of well-oiled, rarely used weaponry, as officers took position to fire on the person whose footsteps approached.

"It's Hetheridge!" the chief superintendent shouted. "Stand down!"

Despite his self-identification, Hetheridge came into view with hands up. Blood and bits of shiny white tissue covered half his face, and for one endless moment Kate thought he'd been shot in the head. Then she realized his eyes were clear and his gait was steady. The fatal wound had been Madge's.

"Tony!"

The restraining hands released her. As Hetheridge tried to wipe his face on his overcoat, Kate threw herself against him, heedless of the gruesome remnants. Emergency technicians rushed into the house, pushing Kate and Hetheridge aside as she scanned him, top to bottom, convinced he bore some hidden wound.

"Are you okay?"

He nodded, taking deep gulps of air.

"Are you mad? Why did you do that?"

Hetheridge didn't speak.

"Why?" Kate screamed.

Hetheridge gripped her hands to silence her, or perhaps to answer her. Staring in his eyes, Kate wasn't sure what passed between them.

Hetheridge's gaze dropped. "Blood."

Kate looked at his legs, then her own. A dark triangle had begun to spread along her left trouser leg. As she watched it grow, mesmerized, her lower back and left side were gripped by vicious, rapidly increasing contractions.

"Oh, no."

"You!" Hetheridge caught a rescue worker by the arm, yanking him toward Kate. "See to her. Now!"

CHAPTER TWENTY-SIX

*H*etheridge knew it was a cliché to detest hospitals, but he didn't so much detest the places as avoid them altogether. During his father's final hospitalization he'd been legitimately—and blessedly—detained on a case that demanded his presence until the day of the funeral. But if Hetheridge had managed a bedside visit, heaven only knew what he and his father would have said to one another. As for his mother, she'd exhibited the good breeding to drop dead at home. Not for her the scuffed linoleum, stark white walls and fluorescent lights that never stopped burning. But if she had been confined to one of these numbered rooms, surrounded by bustling medical personnel, by beeps and whispers and bursts of nervous laughter, what would he have said to her? Hetheridge didn't know. He imagined himself offering a bunch of cellophane-wrapped flowers, struggling to look anything but miserably uncomfortable as he—what? Came forth with a tide of heretofore unexpressed emotion?

Glancing at the cellophane-wrapped bouquet in his hand— yellow and pink flowers pronounced "cheery" by the shopkeeper —Hetheridge made his way through the aseptic-smelling ward to room 6115. Outside the door, on a whiteboard, someone had block-printed in blue marker: K. Wakefield.

What would he say to Kate?

He drew in his breath. This was duty. He could manage duty. At least he had for sixty years, give or take the odd spot of cowardice.

The door was open, and to his relief and frustration, Kate wasn't alone. He'd imagined her in drug-induced slumber, face half-obscured by an oxygen mask, needles and tubes poking out of bruised flesh. Instead he found her propped up against a mound of pillows, wooden board across her lap, playing cards with two young men.

One, a bespectacled blob, he guessed was the nephew, Henry. The other, a tall man with unruly curls, Hetheridge momentarily mistook for an old suitor, à la the late Dylan, who'd seen the news and rushed to Kate's side. A surge of resentment struck him, along with an impulse to drop the bouquet and flee. But then the curly-haired man turned his unflinching, over-direct stare on Hetheridge, and he realized he looked upon Kate's brother, Ritchie.

"Hi, chief," Kate said. Her hair was in need of a wash and her face was uncharacteristically devoid of makeup, but her smile made him clutch the flowers tighter.

"Hallo," he said. Why did she call him "chief" when this was a social call? Why did he care?

"Guys, this is my guv, Chief Superintendent Hetheridge. Chief, this is Henry Wakefield," she indicated the blob, "and this is my brother, Ritchie."

Hetheridge put out his hand to each in turn. "Tony," he muttered. "How do you do?"

"I'm okay," Ritchie said.

"How do you do," Henry said evenly. He surprised Hetheridge with his firm handshake and correct response, which was disappearing so quickly, Hetheridge thought he might live to see its extinction.

"Should we call you Lord Hetheridge?" Henry's eyes sparkled behind large round spectacles. He seemed to hope for an excuse to use the title as much as possible.

"Like Lord Vader," Ritchie said.

"Dark Lord of the Sith!" Henry dropped the mature manner, dissolving into childish laughter that Ritchie promptly joined. Kate rolled her eyes.

"Henry, weren't you going to show Ritch the Canteen? He's still hungry."

"I fancy a sweet," Ritchie told Hetheridge.

"I've shown him already," Henry protested, throwing down his cards.

"Show him again," Kate said. "I know you have a few quid left. Share with Ritchie, and I'll make it up to you later."

Henry digested this command with ill-grace. Indicating Hetheridge with his eyes, he stage whispered, "Ask about the fencing." Then he flounced into the hall, forcing Ritchie to leap up, nearly knocking over Hetheridge in his effort to catch up.

"No, you can't hold my hand!" Henry's indignant voice carried back to the room. "I'm not your boyfriend!"

"They seem in good spirits," Hetheridge said, as he would have remarked about a host's crotch-sniffing dogs.

"Oh, they're charming, all right. And if you're wondering, they have no idea I'm the officer Madge held at gunpoint, or ... what you did. And no clue about the miscarriage, either. They think I'm in for a stomach bug." Kate adopted a bright, not-too-serious tone. "Speaking of what you did. I still haven't thanked you properly."

"I wish you wouldn't."

Kate gathered up the cards, placing the pack and the lap desk atop the bedside table. "You can sit down if you want," she said mildly.

Hetheridge perched on one of the institution-style chairs. The room was too hot. Sweat had begun to roll down his back, a sensation he detested.

"Are those for me?"

Hetheridge looked at Kate blankly.

"The flowers?"

"Oh, yes. Indeed yes, here you are," he heard himself dithering, along with the reflexive throat-clearing he'd so often mocked in his father and grandfather.

Kate gave the bouquet a sniff. "I don't think anyone's given me flowers before. Cheers, guv." She placed the bouquet atop the bedside table. "And speaking of the miscarriage. You must be relieved I didn't whisk you down to the Registry Office the day after you proposed, eh?"

Hetheridge floundered mentally for the right reply. Just as he sensed it within his grasp, Kate said, "No, forget that, it wasn't fair of me to say. You'll have to excuse me. I've come out with some odd remarks since yesterday. I feel like a rubber band stretched too far. Like I might pop."

"You will." Lest he sound too serious, or—heaven forbid—begin confiding the worst moments of his own sleepless night, Hetheridge added, "Just be sure to vent the explosion on an object self-absorbed enough to withstand it. Like DS Bhar."

"He was here this morning. Played Mad Libs with the boys. He mentioned you insisted on prosecuting Kevin Whitley for providing an illegal weapon to Madge. Is this the first hint of fatherly impulses toward Jules?" Kate sounded irritated rather than teasing.

"I don't know. My life used to make sense. Now with the arrival of Jules and, well, other concerns, I'm making decisions moment by moment," Hetheridge said honestly. "Usually I don't personally involve myself in issues relatively tangential to the case, but in this instance—yes. I think the kindest thing I can do for Jules is eliminate the most negative influence in her life."

"That cow will just find someone worse. Not that it matters. Aristocrats never turn on their own. Madge told me that, and I think she was right. Do you suppose that's why she shot herself, instead of you? So you'd be around to mind Jules?"

"Perhaps." Hetheridge sighed. They were back on dangerous ground, heading into topics he would happily pay thousands to sidestep. "You think I shouldn't try to impose myself in Jules's life, then?"

"I think she cold-bloodedly left me to die." Kate blinked a few times, looking away. "If you still want to know her, that's your business."

The silence stretched for so long, Hetheridge seriously considered commenting on the weather. Then inspiration struck. "Charlie Fringate's been cleared of all charges, you know. We're confident Madge lifted his handgun without his knowledge. We'll probably prosecute him at a future date for illegal possession, but not now. He's under suicide watch at this very hospital. Became hysterical when he learned Madge shot herself. Sobbed like a child." His tone held the requisite contempt, even as he added mentally, *the lucky bastard.*

"Lucky bastard," Kate said.

Hetheridge blinked at her. Then he smiled.

"It would be easier, wouldn't it?"

"God, yes."

The sounds of Henry and Ritchie Wakefield preceded their arrival by a good thirty seconds. It was the sort of "you are," "no, you are," banter heard daily in every schoolyard and pub in Britain. Ritchie was eating a Cornetto; Henry had a family-sized bag of cookies. Hetheridge, who deviated from his peers in his dislike of crotch-sniffing, shoe-devouring canines, felt much the same about children and childlike adults. Time to escape.

"When are you due for release, then?" he asked, almost jumping to his feet.

Kate looked amused. "Tomorrow. And I should be back at the Yard in a week or two."

That long? Hetheridge thought. But what did he know about miscarriage? And surely not everyone chose to recover from the threat of violent death by immersing themselves in a fresh murder investigation as soon as possible.

"I'll try not to strangle Bhar while you're gone." Hetheridge moved toward the door as Henry and Ritchie settled back into their chairs. Ritchie was absorbed in his ice cream, and Henry was shoveling down cookies. Kate, replacing the long wooden desk across her lap, began shuffling cards. Hetheridge realized he was obligated to go, he had essentially excused himself, yet he hadn't accomplished his primary goal—settling on a day to see Kate again. One or two weeks was too long to wait.

"So the fencing's all fixed?" Henry said between mouthfuls.

"Oh." Kate slapped her hand against her forehead. "Tony, I'm sorry to ask, but would you be willing to give Henry fencing lessons? He's keen on the notion, especially if you can scare up a lightsaber or two."

Henry made a contemptuous noise. "Nobody's come up with real lightsaber technology yet, Kate."

"My mistake." Kate shot her cheeky grin at Hetheridge, making him realize he would have said yes to anything, including dogsitting.

"I'll be glad to. When can you bring Henry by?" he asked, proud of how neutral he sounded.

"Friday around seven?"

"Friday at seven it is."

Hetheridge strode even faster than usual toward the lifts. He hadn't much time. He needed to arrange for the rental of a portly child's costume and mask. The third-floor loo was dodgy, too. He had to get Harvey on it posthaste, or his Friday guests would surely try to flush too much paper and make it overflow.

As the lift opened, Hetheridge curtailed a boyish impulse to whistle. He knew the specter of the gun would reappear when he tried to sleep that night, as would Madge's expression as she pulled the trigger. But one advantage of turning sixty was the realization that still being alive was the point. Perhaps the Charlie Fringates of the nation, mocked as they were, had the market cornered on emotional expression. That was fine, at least until it ended in a suicide watch. Hetheridge and Kate weren't that sort. They carried on.

He caught himself whistling a scrap of tune as the lift began to descend. The lift's only other passenger, an old trout in a powder blue suit, shot him a look of disapproval. Hetheridge ignored her.

Friday, he thought. The Bentley's driver, seeing him emerge from the hospital, eased the vehicle toward the curb. Putting on his sunglasses, a convenience Hetheridge now couldn't imagine living without, he strode into the daylight.

THE END

ALSO BY EMMA JAMESON

Ice Blue (Lord & Lady Hetheridge #1)

Blue Murder (Lord & Lady Hetheridge #2)

Something Blue (Lord & Lady Hetheridge #3)

Black & Blue (Lord & Lady Hetheridge #4)

Blue Blooded (Lord & Lady Hetheridge #5)

Blue Christmas (Lord & Lady Hetheridge #6)

Deadly Trio: Three English Mysteries (Ice Blue, Blue Murder, Something Blue)

Marriage Can Be Murder (Dr. Benjamin Bones #1)

Divorce Can Be Deadly (Dr. Benjamin Bones #2)

Dr. Bones and the Christmas Wish (Magic of Cornwall #1)

Dr. Bones and the Lost Love Letter (Magic of Cornwall #2)